Also by Scott Allen

Llama United

MACMILLAN CHILDREN'S BOOKS

LLAMAS GO LARGE

SCOTT ALLEN

ILLUSTRATED BY SARAH HORNE

First published 2018 by Macmillan Children's Books
an imprint of Pan Macmillan
20 New Wharf Road, London N1 9RR
Associated companies throughout the world
www.panmacmillan.com

ISBN 978-1-5098-4092-2

Text copyright © Scott Allen 2018
Illustrations copyright © Sarah Horne 2018

The right of Scott Allen and Sarah Horne to be identified as the
author and illustrator of this work has been asserted by them
in accordance with the Copyright, Designs and Patents Act 1988.

1 3 5 7 9 8 6 4 2

A CIP catalogue record for this book is available from
the British Library.

Printed and bound by CPI Group (UK) Ltd, Croydon CR0 4YY

To Spike and Zach —
I knew you when you were babies!

1
THE RETURN

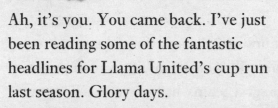

THE BEST CUP FINAL EVER!!!

LLAMAS INCHES AWAY FROM CUP GLORY

LAST-GASP CUP DEFEAT FOR PLUCKY LLAMAS

LEGIT LLAMAS LIKE A BOSS IN FINAL

Ah, it's you. You came back. I've just been reading some of the fantastic headlines for Llama United's cup run last season. Glory days.

What do you mean, you can't remember who I am?

It's me, Arthur Muckluck, the greatest footballer in the world ever! Last year, eleven llamas unknowingly ate my ashes and became brilliant at football. They then went on an amazing cup run, beating all the best human teams around, until they were unfortunately pipped to the post in the final.

You must remember that, now? OK, what about Tim Gravy and Cairo Anderson? Two best friends who managed Llama United all the way to the Cup final. Tim even scored the winning goal in the semi-final, while playing in goal! You really don't remember? It was all over the papers . . .

Well, never mind. I've pretty much told you the story of Llama United now, so you should be up to speed.

Tim, Cairo and the llamas have been really busy since then.

After the Cup final, Llama United started to get requests for friendlies and exhibition matches from some of the biggest teams in the world. They were in so much demand, they didn't have to start playing in a league. In the summer holidays, they travelled to Brazil, the spiritual home of football, and played on the famous Copacabana beach. They arranged a huge match against a team of over one hundred local people and still won 92 – 7. Goal Machine, Llama United's star striker, scored about fifty goals. The game went on for what felt like a whole day, and nobody knew who the referee was. Tim and Cairo had at least ten ice creams each, and felt a bit sick, and McCloud, their grumpy Scottish coach, didn't take his cap or tracksuit off at all, even though it was boiling hot.

Fitting things around school was difficult, but Tim and Cairo trained the llamas every evening and weekend, and in the half-term holidays they all went to Spain to play the giants of Borcaloona and Royal Modrid. Llama United defender Bill did do a poo in one of the star player's boots, but he didn't notice until he got home that night. He needs to buy a new carpet now.

At Christmas the whole team were invited to play in China. The Duke, Goal Machine and Smasher did headers and volleys over the Great Wall of China. Some schoolchildren tried to teach Cruncher how to play ping-pong, but he was only interested in eating the net. Tim and Cairo drank some yak's milk. Let's just say they won't be putting it on their cereal in the morning.

And in the Easter holidays, the llamas were granted

3

an audience with the Pope in his home in the Vatican City, a tiny state hiding in a corner of Rome. Cruncher chewed the edge of his cassock when he was blessing the llamas' noses. Thankfully, the Pope laughed and let him chew on his *zucchetto*, which is that small white hat he sometimes wears when he is doing all that waving at people. Like Popes tend to do. After all the waving, Tim and Cairo ate a lot of the best pizza they had ever tasted, and not one slice had any pineapple on it. Because we all know that's wrong, don't we?

Tim, Cairo and their grumpy Scottish coach, McCloud, had followed the llamas around the world, and though they had enjoyed every minute, it was incredibly exhausting. Tim's dad, Frank, also came on all the trips, because McCloud is as good at looking after two children and eleven llamas as I am at French. *Benjure, monsewer, je apple Arthur, silver plate.*

One day, on the way back from a short weekend trip to Germany, where Goal Machine had smashed five past the German champions Booyern Moonich, Cairo noticed that Tim looked a bit fed up. He'd hardly touched his 'delicious' airline meal of a brown meat-paste sandwich, a tiny orange juice and a dry brownie, and was staring blankly out of the window. He certainly wasn't thinking about what type of meat was in the brown paste. Shrew, perhaps?

'You OK, gaffer?' asked Cairo. 'You seem a bit down. Is everything all right?'

Tim let out a deep sigh. Clearly, everything wasn't OK. However, because he's a boy, and twelve, he said: 'Yep, everything is great. All good.'

Then he went back to staring out the window again.

Cairo, because he is also a boy, and twelve, shrugged and didn't press his friend any more. He picked up a magazine from the back of the chair in front of him and began reading about a cheese-flavoured chocolate bar that was being made in South Africa. Yuck! Within minutes he was fast asleep.

2
LUDO THE AGONY AUNT

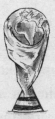

That evening, after dinner at the farm where Tim lived with his mum, dad and two sisters, Tim went out to the new state-of-the-art training ground, built with all the money they had made from being famous.

The llamas were all tucked up in their shed, having a sleep after their travels. He began dribbling a ball up and down the pitch, weaving in and out of a handful of cones that had been left out. For a goalkeeper, he had pretty good control.

Tim wasn't really sure why he felt so low, but something was knocking away, deep in the pit of his stomach. He couldn't talk to his parents, sisters, McCloud or Cairo. They would just think he was being selfish. He had everything he could ever want, so what was wrong with him?

As the sun was substituted for the moon, Tim could just make out a tall, dark figure striding purposefully out of the early evening gloom. Tim smiled as it got closer. It was Ludo, Llama United's brilliant goalkeeper, and if I'm honest, my favourite player – well, one of my favourite players. I'm also quite keen on Goal Machine . . . oh, and Smasher, and maybe Barcelona. Actually, I like them all, really.

Ludo looked majestic as ever, nothing ever phased him. He was what every manager in the world wants from a keeper, unflappable, strong and focused. Ludo wasn't interested in many things, apart from grass, football and protecting Llama United's goalmouth sheep, Motorway, who thought she was a princess.

Tim reached up and stroked Ludo under the chin. It was his favourite place to be stroked. He then let out a deep, mournful sigh. Tim, not Ludo. Ludo never sighed. Although he sometimes liked to hum.

'Oh, Ludo,' said Tim. 'What's wrong with me? I have no idea why I feel so unhappy. I just do, and I shouldn't. I've got everything I could ever want.'

Ludo stared deep into Tim's eyes. Neither of them blinked for what seemed like an age. Actually it was eleven seconds, but it always feels longer, doesn't it?

Tim blinked first. Ludo lowered his head and took a huge bite out of the lush green turf beneath their feet and began casually chewing on it. Of all the llamas in

the team, he had the best manners. Bob ate with his mouth wide open so you could see exactly what he was mushing around his mouth. It wasn't very pleasant.

'The world tour was fantastic, wasn't it?'

Ludo carried on chewing and didn't reply.

'It was really, really good. But it was missing something. We met celebrities and world–class footballers, but it just wasn't the Cup, was it?'

Ludo carried on chewing and still didn't reply.

'The Cup had a sort of magic to it. Something we didn't have during the tour.'

Ludo looked at Tim, and then swallowed his mouthful. His neck swung low to the ground and he took another bite out of the turf. If you think Ludo is going to start talking, then I'm afraid you've got another think coming. He's a llama, after all. Tim watched Ludo's jaw go round and round and round as he munched on the grass. It was almost hypnotic. Then something in his brain flashed.

'Of course, that's it!' he said, slapping his forehead. 'There's no competition.'

Ludo carried on chewing.

'There's no pressure on us; we don't have anything to aim for. Nobody cares if we win, draw or lose all these friendly matches; they just help the clubs we play to make more money because we're famous. None of it really matters. We have all this training stuff and no real plan about what we're doing next, and nobody gets to see your true talent when you're not under pressure in a proper match.'

Ludo paused . . . and snorted.

'We need to play in some important matches again, Ludo. We need to win a massive, big, shiny, silver trophy. You'd like that, wouldn't you?'

Ludo sniffed and swallowed his latest mouthful. He wasn't one for dramatic reactions.

'Oh, thanks, Ludo, you've totally helped me figure this out,' said Tim, as a broad grin spread across his face. 'I couldn't have done it without you.'

He gave Ludo a big hug round the neck.

Ludo gazed off into the distance, and began sucking at his teeth to try and remove all the grass that was caught between them. Tim tickled him under the chin one more time, turned on his heel and marched across to the little caravan that was parked behind the training pitch. A surge of energy pulsed through Tim's body. He felt alive again.

He was going to see McCloud.

Which sounds more impressive than it actually is. He only lives on the other side of the training ground.

3
SCOUTING MCCLOUD

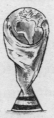

Tim knocked loudly three times on McCloud's caravan door. Nothing.

He knocked again and then pressed his ear to the door to see if he could hear anything from inside. He was greeted by total silence. This was odd. When McCloud wasn't travelling with the team, he was usually in one of two places. When he was awake he was on the training pitch, talking about football, and when he was asleep he was in his caravan, dreaming about football. Tim couldn't remember a time he wasn't in these places. Loving football so much gave McCloud a very curious and unpredictable view on life. You were not to be trusted if you didn't like football, and everyone who did like football couldn't be trusted either. *Trust no one*, that was his motto. Apart from maybe Tim, Cairo and the llamas. Although he didn't like the way the Duke looked at him.

A cold feeling covered Tim's shoulders like a wet towel. What if McCloud was ill, had fallen over, or worse still, had gone in search of the mythical tartan paint? He always said this was a journey of no return.

Tim began knocking and frantically pulling on the tiny plastic door handle, a whoosh of worry surging through his body.

'MCCLOUD,' he shouted through the thin door. 'Can you hear me, MCCLOUD? . . . Are you OK?'

He peered though the murky windows. All had orange curtains tightly drawn across them. Only one small light glowed from the inside.

'MCCLOUD, MCCLOUD, MC . . . CLOUD!!!' barked Tim, thumping the sides of the caravan with his closed fists. He was really panicking now.

There was a sharp cough from behind him. Tim spun round.

'Flaming tangerines, what's all this fuss, laddie?' It was McCloud. He was dressed, as usual, in his blue velvet Scotland tracksuit. Although his face was smeared in black, green and brown face paint and he had twigs and branches sticking out of

his flat cap. Which was unusual. He looked like a soldier in the jungle. Well, his head did. The rest of him looked like an old football coach.

The fear drained from Tim in an instant when he saw his wiry Scottish coach.

'Where have you been? I was worried.'

'I've been out,' replied McCloud, tapping the side of his green camouflaged nose and looking about suspiciously.

'Out where?' asked Tim. 'You never go out.'

'Sometimes a coach has to go out.' McCloud tapped the side of his nose again. The green camouflage face paint was now transferring from his nose to his fingers.

'But where?'

'I cannae tell you, it's a secret.'

Tim rolled his eyes. He knew McCloud was rubbish at keeping secrets, but he had a special tactic to make the Scottish coach reveal them almost straight away.

'OK,' he said, with a shrug of his shoulders. 'I'm going in now, it's getting late, and I've got a milkshake at home that won't drink itself.'

'Fine, fine,' said McCloud quickly. 'You've twisted my arm . . . . I'll tell you.'

Tim knew McCloud hated being ignored.

'I've been out scouting,' whispered McCloud, sneaking a glance over his own shoulder.

'Scouting?' asked Tim doubtfully, peering over McCloud's shoulder to see what he was looking at.

'Shh, keep it down, will you?' exclaimed McCloud, grabbing Tim and pulling him behind a bush.

'You don't need to dress up in camouflage gear to go scouting,' said Tim. 'You can just go and watch matches whenever you want. It doesn't have to be a secret.'

'Doesn't it?' said McCloud with a knowing wink and another tap of his nose.

'No, it doesn't,' replied Tim. 'Anyway, why are you scouting? We don't have any competitive matches coming up.'

McCloud's shoulders slumped. 'I know, laddie. That's the problem. I'm missing the cut 'n' thrust of important matches. It's great playing and beating all the best teams in the world, but everyone is just so happy about it all – it doesnae really matter if we win, lose or draw. I thought a bit of secretive scouting might make me feel better . . . but it hasn't.'

Tim's eyes widened. McCloud was feeling exactly the same as he was! They both missed playing serious matches.

'I know how you feel,' admitted Tim with a sigh.

'Ye do, laddie?' replied McCloud. A broad grin began to creep across his face.

'That's why I came to find you.'

'Well dunk me in a jam tart, what are we going to do about it then?' asked McCloud. 'It's too late to enter the Cup or the league or a big European competition, the season is nearly over. That team Nork Town has nearly won the league.'

Tim tutted and shook his head at the mention of Nork Town. The team that had kicked, fouled and bullied their way to the top of the league. Llama United played attacking football with style and flair. Nork Town were the total opposite.

'Well, I was wondering . . .' Tim said hesitantly. 'How about the World Cup? It's only a few months away.'

'Pffftttt, dinnae be stupid,' replied McCloud. 'It's a team of llamas, not a country. Besides aren't all llamas from South America? They'd have to play for one of those countries. Like Brazil, Peru or Switzerland.'

'Switzerland isn't in South America.'

'Isn't it?' replied McCloud tapping the side of his nose again.

'No, it isn't. It's in the middle of Europe, surrounded by mountains.'

'Aye, that's what they'd like you to think,' said McCloud, knowingly. 'They are tricky, those Swiss, with their chocolate, cuckoo clocks and tortilla crisps.'

Tim shook his head. Tortilla crisps weren't Swiss. They were from South America, weren't they? But he couldn't be bothered to argue with McCloud as it always made it worse.

'Brazil, Peru and Switzerland have already qualified for the World Cup and have strong, settled teams. However, the England team is rubbish. The worst England team in living memory, though I've not been alive very long,' said Tim.

'They've always been rubbish to me,' muttered the Scotsman under his breath.

'I think we should offer the llamas to the England manager, to help boost the squad. They can't do any worse than the current players, who all seem to play for . . . Nork Town,' said Tim, angrily firing out the name of his most hated team.

McCloud grumpily stuffed his hands deep into his tracksuit trouser pockets.

'And why can't we offer Scotland some of the

15

llamas?' he said grumpily. 'They need just as much help.'

'Well, they are English llamas, they live and were raised in England, so they wouldn't qualify to play for Scotland,' said Tim firmly. And then, more apologetically, 'Besides . . . Scotland haven't qualified.'

McCloud kicked at the grass and muttered something very rude under his breath. As a proud Scotsman, helping out England was something you weren't supposed to do. A bit like wearing the shirt of your rival football team or putting ketchup on a roast dinner. However, for McCloud, the pull of big important football matches was too much.

After a long pause, and some more muttering, McCloud said, 'Ach, Hibees, I suppose, if it means we get to play competitive football again, then I'm willing to give it a shot. Getting llamas to a World Cup, though . . . could be tricky.' McCloud, rubbed his chin.

'Nah, all we've got to do now is persuade the England manager to pick them in his World Cup squad. I'm sure he'll be glad of the help.'

You'll notice this book is full of bold statements like this. They usually turn out to be wrong.

4
THE ENGLAND BOSS

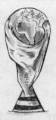

Tim was right. England were a terrible team. They had failed miserably at the last handful of World Cups and European Championships and had a selection of very average players wearing the famous shirt.

The current manager was called Ray Barnowl. Not only did he look like a barn owl, his head could almost turn 360 degrees and he also liked eating dormice . . . All right, I might have made that last bit up.

As a club manager, he hadn't won any major trophies, apart from Best Manager's Nose Hair at the World Manager of the Year awards, so it was a big surprise that he had been given the top England job . . . although it was lovely nose hair. Things didn't go much better for him after that. The players he picked were very ordinary, and when they played together they were a shambles.

One thing Barnowl *did* have was luck. The matches

that England won were usually down to luck rather than the skill of the team. An own goal here, a dodgy penalty there, or a pigeon heading home the winner against Sweden in a World Cup qualifying match.

This wasn't the pigeon's intention, by the way. He was flying home after a long day working with the tourists at Trafalgar Square and decided to take a short cut via Wombley Stadium. The pigeon was called Jeff, if you are interested. As he swooped down across the pitch, a long-range shot from one of the England defenders caught the startled Jeff square on the beak and looped in over the Swedish keeper's head, straight into the back of the net. England 1 – 0 Sweden!

Having qualified for the World Cup, Ray Barnowl was expecting to be hailed as a hero. But the fans were fed up with him and his team's string of boringly lucky results. They didn't want to be embarrassed at *another* World Cup.

So the fans did what they do best: BOO!!! Barnowl was booed everywhere he went, making leaving his house a real problem. The players were booed at their clubs, while they were training, and even when they went out for dinner. There was a Best Booing championship on TV, which was won by someone

called Simon.
Barnowl hardly
slept and spent
most nights
wandering
round his house
in his green
dressing gown,
worrying.
When he did
finally go to bed he

would sleep with one eye open, and dream about people booing him. He wasn't actually dreaming about booing – it was his wife lying next to him in bed, booing gently into his ear.

The England team were a massive joke. They made it even worse by losing their World Cup warm-up friendlies to some of the smallest countries in the world – Liechtenstein, Malta and Barbados. Barnowl appeared to have lost control, so it was the perfect opportunity for Tim and McCloud to approach the manager with their llama proposal. Time was running out, the World Cup was getting closer and closer.

5
FINDING BARNOWL

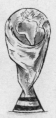

The media was hounding Barnowl at every opportunity. Between boos, they asked if he was going to resign, so, unsurprisingly, Barnowl decided he should go into hiding.

Unfortunately, Barnowl wasn't very good at hiding. Tucking himself behind the large, thick red curtain in his office at England headquarters seemed like the next best idea. Which it wasn't.

Barnowl was standing behind the curtain for the third day in a row when Tim, Cairo, McCloud and Tim's annoying little sister Fiona arrived at England headquarters to talk to him. Fiona claimed she was easily the best negotiator in the world, so had to be there.

Frank sat in the car with the engine running. It's very hard to park in central London.

Fiona reached up and pressed the large gold buzzer on the front door. She had put herself in charge of 'pushing important buttons'.

'Hello, England headquarters,' answered a posh voice.

'Oh, hello, it's Tim, Cairo, McCloud and, er . . . Fiona from Llama United. We were wondering if we could have a word with the England manager,' said Tim in his most polite voice ever.

'Do you have an appointment?' came the bored-sounding voice from the gold speaker.

Tim and Cairo gave each other a worried look. Nobody had thought to ring ahead.

'Yes, we have an appointment,' said Fiona boldly. 'I was also promised mango juice during the meeting.'

There was a shuffling of papers and a muttering from behind the gold speaker.

'I'm afraid the England manager is away on a scouting mission at the moment,' lied the voice eventually. 'So you'd have to rearrange the visit.'

'No, he isn't,' said Fiona. 'I can see him hiding behind the curtain on the second floor. He is wearing a jacket and no trousers. He has very hairy legs.'

Barnowl didn't always dress like this, but he'd just spilt a load of tomato ketchup on his trousers and

he'd sent them off to be washed.

Through the gold speaker came the shuffling of more papers and more muttering.

'Sorry, he's not here,' said the now flustered voice, and the speaker was turned off.

'Oh,' said Tim disappointedly. 'That wasn't very nice.'

'This is England HQ,' muttered McCloud. 'What do you expect? You cannae just rock up, like a wee badger in a top hat.'

Tim gave McCloud a curious look, but didn't ask about the badger.

A large brown paper bag full of tomatoes was suddenly shoved under Tim's nose. Fiona was holding them.

'Tomatoes?' said Tim slowly. 'Where did you get them from?'

Fiona turned and pointed at the fruit and veg stall on the other side of road. The man on the stall gave Tim a thumbs-up and shouted, 'Love your llamas. Help yourself, got plenty of stuff here.'

'Now we hurl the tomatoes at Barnowl's window,' said Fiona gleefully, cocking her wrist and launching a huge red tomato at the side of the England HQ building.

'WHHHHEEEEEEEE SPLAAAAATTTTTT,' said the tomato as it flew through the air and exploded on the wall just below Barnowl's window. Tomatoes love being thrown, it's so much better than being eaten.

'Hey, whoa! Whoa!' shouted Tim, grabbing his sister's arm, trying to stop her. 'You can't go throwing tomatoes at someone's window.'

'WHHHHEEEEEEEE SPLAAAAAAATTTT,' said a different tomato, launched by McCloud. He had a much better aim than Fiona and it hit smack bang in the middle of the glass with an incredibly satisfying squelch.

'Hey! McCloud!' shouted Cairo. 'You can't do that.'

'Can't I?' replied McCloud with a menacing stare, grabbing another large tomato. 'I can do what I like. I'm an old man.'

'PINNNNGGGG TINNNNNNGGGG,' came a different noise.

'Lychees,' said Cairo, holding the fat bullet-shaped fruit in the air.

'WILL EVERYONE JUST STOP,' shouted Tim at the top of his voice. 'THIS ISN'T RIGHT. They'll never listen to us if we're throwing things. Would *you*?'

Cairo, McCloud and Fiona looked down at the street and guiltily put the fruit back in the brown paper bags.

'I've got a pineapple you can have,' called the fruit and veg seller chirpily. Tim ignored him.

The window on the second floor opened and Barnowl's head slowly and nervously poked through it.

'Stop throwing fruit!' he shouted.

'We have,' replied Tim. 'I'm sorry, your receptionist wouldn't let us in and we needed to speak to you.'

'Let us in, Mr Barnowl!' shouted Fiona.

Tim quickly put his hand over her mouth to stop her from saying anything that would make Barnowl shut the window.

'People have been throwing fruit at my window for weeks now, thanks to him.' Barnowl pointed at the man in the fruit stall across the road. The man waved back, and did another thumbs-up.

'We're really sorry,' said Tim. 'We just wanted to talk about the World Cup, we think we can help.'

'How?'

'With our llamas. We're from Llama United.'

'Why don't you let us in so we can talk about it a

24

bit more?' called Cairo, sensing that Barnowl might be interested in their llama plan.

Barnowl's gaze moved from Tim across to Cairo, whom he hadn't really noticed before. Then his eyes fell on McCloud, standing there in his blue Scotland tracksuit. His face immediately changed, as though his ears had sucked a dark storm cloud into the rest of his head.

'YOU!!!' Barnowl barked accusingly at McCloud, his face going purple. Then he slammed the window shut without saying another word.

Tim, Cairo and Fiona stared at McCloud, his hands firmly planted in his pockets as though he was watching the first fifteen minutes of a Llama United match. He was showing all the emotion of a block of concrete.

'What was that?' asked Tim.

'I've nae idea,' replied McCloud with a shrug.

'Oh, c'mon,' added Cairo. 'Barnowl clearly knows who you are, and doesn't like you.'

'Beats me, laddie,' replied McCloud with another ice-cold shrug. 'Perhaps he dinnae like a successful Scotsman.'

'Oh, McCloud . . .' said Tim with a resigned sigh. He knew getting McCloud to open up was impossible.

McCloud kept his personal feelings in a small bottle, at the bottom of the deepest loch.

Frank pulled up in the car. He looked stressed, like most dads do when they have to do driving in a busy city.

'Are you lot done yet?' he called through the window. 'I've been driving round the block for ages now and I've got loads of traffic wardens chasing me. Quick, jump in.'

Tim stared blankly at shops and offices as Frank's car lurched slowly through the clogged streets of the capital. Why had Barnowl suddenly changed his mood when he saw McCloud? Something fishy was going on. There had to be another way of getting to the England manager. But how?

'Er . . . where's Fiona?' asked Frank with a squawk, spinning round in his seat.

Tim and Cairo looked nervously at each other.

'Erm . . . I don't actually know,' said Tim.

6
FIONA THE NINJA

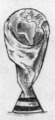

'Barnowl.' The word softly echoed from the corner of the England manager's office.

Ray Barnowl peered out into the darkness of his office. As he was in hiding, he didn't bother turning the lights on any more. This meant he was constantly stubbing his big toe and whacking into furniture.

'Barnowl,' came the soft voice again, this time slightly closer.

'Er . . . hello?' replied Barnowl nervously in the darkness. He began fumbling around on his desk for something heavy to protect himself with. All he could find was a half-eaten cheese-and-onion baguette left over from yesterday's lunch.

'Who's there?' he asked again, holding his baguette aloft like a sword. He'd received plenty of threats, and had people hurling stuff at his window, over the past few weeks, but his security was so tight, surely nobody could get into his office like this.

'I'm going to call security,' said Barnowl bravely, fumbling for the red alarm button under his desk. It was dead. Someone had removed the battery.

'Barnowl,' came the voice again. This time from behind his chair.

He spun his chair around. A bright torch light was shone directly into his face, blinding him instantly.

He put his hands over his head and began whimpering. 'Please don't hurt me,' he begged.

The main office light snapped on. As he slowly regained his sight, Barnowl peered through the gap in his fingers to see a figure standing in front of him, dressed from head to toe in black. The person wasn't very big at all.

'How did you get in?' asked Barnowl with a splutter. 'Security should have stopped you. Small ninjas aren't allowed in here.'

The pint-sized figure removed the black hood that was covering its face.

'YOU!!!' exclaimed Barnowl, looking directly at a grinning Fiona.

'Yes, me,' said Fiona proudly. 'Fiona Gravy – the ninja, and also sometimes a princess.'

'What do you want from me?' asked Barnowl, regaining his composure.

'Well, if my brother was here, he'd ask nicely if you could pick our llamas for the World Cup squad.'

'Oh would he?' replied Barnowl. 'And what would you ask?'

'I'd ask the same thing, but not as nicely.' Fiona brought herself up to her full height, which wasn't actually that tall. 'PICK THE LLAMAS,' she bellowed.

Barnowl rubbed his chin for a few seconds. All football managers do this when they are thinking.

'Why *should* I pick the llamas for my World Cup squad?' he asked eventually.

Fiona let out a huge sigh. 'One, your team is rubbish. Two, everybody knows the llamas are the best players in the world and they'll hate you if you don't pick them. And five, I'll tell everyone about your unicorn pants if you don't.'

'Oh . . . these are my lucky pants,' said Barnowl sheepishly, looking down. He quickly grabbed a newspaper and covered his underwear. 'Everyone hates me already,' he continued glumly. 'I get booed everywhere I go, and I have to hide in this office.'

'They won't hate you if you pick the llamas.'

'But I can't.'

'Why not?' asked Fiona.

'It's difficult to explain. I'd need to talk to a few people first.' Barnowl began fiddling nervously with the handle on his desk drawer.

'Who?' asked Fiona. 'I thought you were the England manager.'

'I am,' replied Barnowl, adjusting his tie. 'But picking the England squad takes a lot of thinking, and talking to other important people. Erm . . . I mean *I* have to . . . erm, do a lot of . . . erm, thinking. It's all done by me, of course. Nobody else is involved.'

His faced flushed pink and he mopped a bead of sweat off his forehead.

Fiona looked at Barnowl quizzically. He was clearly hiding something. Was the selection of the England squad actually down to him?

Just then there was a screech of brakes, the frantic honk of a car horn and then an anxious shout of

'FIONA, FIONA, FIONA' from outside. It was Frank, looking for his daughter.

'I have to go,' Fiona said quickly. 'It's easy, pick the llamas and everyone will be happy with you again and nobody will find out about your unicorn pants. Don't be an idiot-face.'

She flicked off the main light in the room, there was a little bit of scuffling in the darkness and then she was gone. Almost as quickly as she had arrived. She really was a ninja princess.

Later that night, the kitchen was dark apart from the glow of a computer on the table at the end of the room. Tim's elder sister Monica was hunched over it, typing furiously. She was sending messages to the media in every way she could think of. Llama United had made friends with loads of journalists, radio shows, bloggers, vloggers and TV programmes since they'd reached the Cup final, and Monica was calling in some favours.

'ARRRGGGGHHHHHH,' she screamed, as a small figure dressed head to toe in black appeared next to her. The figure didn't say anything or move, which made it even scarier, so Monica screamed again.

'AARRRRRGGGGGGHHHHHHH.'

The dark figure reached and peeled off its black mask. A clump of blonde hair tumbled out to reveal the grinning face of Fiona.

'Did you wet your pants?' she crowed.

Monica tutted and carried on typing into her laptop. 'I'm really busy, Fiona. Can we do this another time?'

'What do you think of my new look? I've stopped being a princess and now I'm a ninja,' said Fiona.

Monica smiled weakly and carried on typing.

'What are you doing?' asked Fiona, totally ignoring her sister's request, like younger sisters tend to do.

'I'm working.'

'What you working on?'

'Things.'

'What *things* are you working on?'

'Just things, OK? Too complicated for you to understand.'

'*What* things that are too complicated for seven-year-olds are you working on?'

Monica growled under her breath. Fiona could carry on this kind of conversation forever, especially if it meant she could delay going to bed. She took a deep breath.

'Tim told me you didn't have much luck with Barnowl at England HQ, so I'm sending messages to lots of media places so they can tell everyone that we are offering the England team our brilliant llamas. Hopefully that will make Barnowl change his mind when he's picking the squad.'

'I also had an idea,' said Fiona importantly. 'Which was much better than yours.'

'Whatever,' replied Monica with a huff, turning back to her computer. Then she stopped, and adjusted her glasses.

'What do you mean . . . *was?*'

Fiona grinned, showing her teeth, which had a red tinge to them. She'd found some strawberry liquorice in a drawer and scoffed the whole pack straight after dinner.

'Oh, don't worry, I've already talked to Barnowl,' she said happily. 'He'll change his mind.'

Monica folded her arms and stared at her little sister. *She* was the supposed to be clever one in the family who solved all the problems, not Fiona.

'Should I still carry on with my media campaign, your majesty?' said Monica, pointing at all the hard work on her computer.

Fiona stroked her chin thoughtfully. 'Well, I'm

sure it will help too, but probably not as good as the stuff I've done already.'

She patted her older sister on the head, and skipped out of the room.

Monica pursed her lips, snorted and returned to her screen, muttering under her breath.

Monica's expert work on her laptop got the media firmly on side within hours, and by the next morning, there were hundreds of camera crews camped outside Barnowl's house and England HQ demanding answers about why the llamas weren't being considered for the England World Cup squad. Every page of every newspaper and sports website was devoted to the story.

Huge mobs of people stalked the streets, chanting 'LLAMAS IN', 'PICK THE LLAMAS' and 'OOOH-AHHH, LLAAMAARR, I said OOOH-AHHH, LLAAMAARR'. The songs weren't very imaginative.

But surely Barnowl couldn't ignore the llamas now?

7
BACK TO TRAINING

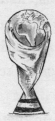

Tim stood on the new training pitch and watched a gaggle of clumsy-looking men in jeans and T-shirts stagger on to the pitch. McCloud was leading the way.

Yesterday, Fiona had told Tim that Barnowl might change his mind about having llamas in the England team. It took a while for him to work out what Fiona actually meant, because for about an hour she just stood beside him winking secretly.

'Here they are then,' said McCloud, pointing at the group of men. 'White Horse FC, in all their glory.' Tim could tell McCloud was not impressed with the team from the village, especially as none of them were wearing proper kit.

'You've not got us for long, cos we've got to get to the pub for quiz night,' said one of the White Horse players.

Knowing that the llamas might be added to the England line-up, especially with the pressure now coming from the media, had set the tiny cogs in Tim's brain whirring. He knew that *all* of Llama United wouldn't be picked – no international manager ever chose an entire team for their squad. So that left a problem: the llamas had never played with humans on the same team before. They'd only ever played *against* them. So Tim decided to run a few experiments with White Horse FC. The last thing he wanted was the England players and the llamas clashing before the World Cup had even started.

Tim mixed a few White Horse players into the Llama United team, and placed himself, Cairo, his mum (Beetroot), Frank, and Cairo's mum (Molly) into the rest of the White Horse team. Cairo and Frank weren't very good at football, but the two mums were rocket quick and had loads of stamina, so they would probably be some of the best players on the pitch. McCloud would referee, while Monica would live-stream the game for social media. Fiona had disappeared again, which she did all the time now, so it wasn't much of a surprise.

McCloud peeped his whistle and the game got going. As Tim had feared, the llamas had no interest in passing to any of the White Horse players on their team. For the first half, it was all llama. Tim was very busy in goal for the human team, making save after save from shots by Llama United's stars Goal Machine and Lightning. Despite his best efforts it was 5 – 0 at half-time. Goal Machine had scored a hat-trick, and Cruncher and the Duke had netted the other two. At the other end, Ludo the Llama United keeper and the goalmouth sheep Motorway stood munching grass and looking bored. Motorway even fell asleep for ten minutes.

Tim wasn't worried about this. He was worried that the llamas didn't involve the White Horse players in their team, who were starting to get very angry about not getting a touch of the ball. The llamas would be no good in the England team if they were going to be this selfish.

Cairo wandered over to Tim at half-time looking exhausted, even though he had hardly done a thing.

'Think I'm getting any better?' he asked. 'I think I'm really improving as a player.'

'Erm, slightly,' lied Tim. He didn't want to tell his friend he was still the worst player he had ever met.

'Why not mix the teams up again?' suggested Cairo. 'I've got a tactic.'

'Really? You? . . . Tactics?' spluttered Tim.

'Yes, really. I can have tactics too,' replied Cairo firmly. 'It's not just you and McCloud who should do all the tactics. After all, the llamas are my speciality.'

Tim was surprised that Cairo looked so annoyed. He'd never frowned at him like that before.

'Put people the llamas know together, not the White Horse players. The llamas have no idea who they are. Swap me, your dad and mum into the Llama United team. They need to get used to playing with humans they trust.'

'But you guys are rubbish,' said Tim unkindly. 'Only Mum will be able to keep up with them.' As soon as the words left Tim's mouth, he knew this was the wrong thing to say. Cairo's face fell.

'Oh, that's what you really think of me, is it? Rubbish?' said Cairo sulkily.

'No, no, no, I didn't mean it like that,' replied Tim, quickly trying to dig himself out of a hole. 'I . . . erm . . . I . . .' He couldn't think of anything to say.

'Just makes the changes. It'll work,' said Cairo as he grumpily stomped back on to the pitch.

'Sorrreeeee, I didn't mean it,' called Tim after his friend, but Cairo wasn't listening.

Tim made the changes, and Cairo was bang on with his prediction. Beetroot found herself in a space on the edge of the area and signalled for a pass from Dasher, who immediately zipped the ball through to her. Beetroot's first-time shot unluckily went over the crossbar, but it proved that Cairo's tactic would work. The llamas had to know and like the humans they were playing with. Tim had to get the llamas and the England team to bond – if they were picked in the squad, of course.

A Goal Machine volley, a Brian header and a fantastic thirty-yarder from Cruncher made the score 8 – 0. Then, with five minutes left, Tim had one of the most embarrassing moments of his life.

Lightning made a lung-busting run down the right, and sent in a lovely looping cross. Tim came out to claim the ball but only managed to fumble it straight into the path of . . . his mum! Beetroot gleefully smashed the ball into the back of the net to make the score 9 – 0. She ran up to Tim and gave him one of those embarrassing kisses mums sometimes do in public.

'Muuuuuuuuummmmmmm,' shouted Tim, as he tried to battle his way out of his mum's embrace.

'Olé, olé, olé, olé, nine–nil, nine–nil,' she crowed

into Tim's ear, and then ran off to celebrate with Frank and Cairo.

'The people online really loved that! A thousand likes already,' shouted Monica across the pitch, holding her laptop above her head, which made Tim feel even worse. At least now they would know what to do if the llamas were selected for the England squad. He just hoped Barnowl would change his mind.

8
SQUAD SELECTION

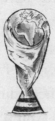

'Yes, I know,' muttered Barnowl miserably into the bright red phone on his desk. 'I'm sorry, I'm really sorry . . . I don't think I have a choice. If I don't do this, I might get the sack and then that could leave big problems for you and some of the rest of the squad.'

He paused and listened to the voice at the other end of the phone. I'm not going to tell you who it is, because I don't know. I can't be in two places at once.

'It will be OK, I think,' he continued, while fiddling with the handle of his drawer again. 'It will help get the media and the whole country off my back . . . You have to trust me this once . . . please.'

The voice at the other end of the phone sounded furious. No, I still don't know who it is.

'OK . . . OK . . . Please don't get angry with me. I understand. I'll only select a few of them, I promise.'

Barnowl put the phone down, put his head in his

hands and let out a long, low sigh.

A large, ripe avocado splatted against his window, followed by two little gem lettuces, which just bounced away unbroken.

This was it, squad selection day, and a large crowd had assembled outside. The fruit and veg seller was doing a roaring trade. If Barnowl didn't pick at least one llama in his World Cup squad, he'd probably be dunked in strawberry jam, coated in cabbage leaves and then made to work as a scarecrow.

Barnowl took a pen out of his drawer and began scribbling on a piece of paper. Ten minutes later he had a list of nineteen names in front of him. World Cup squads are usually made up of twenty-three players and Barnowl had four blank spaces.

1. Pete Badger (GK) Nork Town
2. T. J. Wilkinson (RB) Enfield Hotspurts
3. Steve Crispy (LB) Chulski
4. Paul Peacock (CB) Nork Town
5. Sid Melonhead (CB) Looverpoo
6. Greg Punch (captain) (CDM) Nork Town
7. Preston Cheeks (CB) Nork Town
8. Leo Hedgetrimmer (RW) Munchester United
9. Dwain Drain (CM) Beverton

10. Jack Chilly (ST) Nork Town
11. Mo Moleface (LW) East Ham
12. Russell Brussell (CB/CM) Gunerall
13. Eustace Useless (CB/LB/RB) Munchester City
14. Jim Hoisin (CAM) Nork Town
15. Pete Tart (CM) Munchester City
16. JuJu Tablecloth (CAM) Royal Modrid
17. Phil Monk-Bertgoose (GK) Loods United
18. Chaz Steakhouse (CM/LCM/RCM) Enfield Hotspurts
19. Jo Hussain-Bolt (ST) Nork Town
20.
21.
22.
23.

Barnowl let out another long, deep sigh and pressed a button on his phone that let him speak directly to his secretary in the office next door.

'Hi, Susan, can you get me the manager of Llama United on the phone, please?' said Barnowl.

'That McCloud person?' asked Susan perkily. 'Don't you hate him?' She said everything perkily, even words like 'tired' and 'miserable'.

'Yes, of course I hate him.' Barnowl wistfully rubbed his right kneecap. 'Don't ring him, ring that boy, Tim. He seems like the sensible one.'

Susan, spent a few minutes finding the number in a large book of football contacts, then picked up the phone and rang the number of the Gravy farm.

9
THE CHOSEN ONES

Tim put the phone down and started laughing. The llamas were going to go to the World Cup! Just four though; England needed an extra keeper (Ludo), a winger (Lightning), a midfielder (Cruncher) and a striker (Goal Machine). Tim had managed to persuade Barnowl to agree to let them take him as the llamas' coach, Cairo as the physio, Motorway the goalkeeper's sheep, and even McCloud too. Barnowl was really not keen on McCloud coming, but Tim stayed firm: no McCloud, no llamas. He was getting good at his football negotiation skills.

Just as Tim was doing an excited dance by the phone, Cairo burst into the room with his hands cupped together. He was hopping up and down as though he needed a wee.

'Look! I've got a baby hedgehog!' he shouted excitedly. 'I found it by the side of the training

pitch. I think it's in a bad way.'

He slowly unclasped his hands and Tim cautiously peered inside. It was tiny, pink and covered in spines. Apart from the llamas, Tim still wasn't that fussed about animals.

'I've got some big news,' said Tim, ignoring the baby hedgehog.

'I've got a baby hedgehog, can't it wait?'

'Nope,' replied Tim. 'This is bigger than a baby hedgehog.'

'Everything is bigger than a baby hedgehog.'

'Can you stop saying "baby hedgehog"?' asked Tim impatiently. He was getting annoyed now and he wanted to share his big news with someone before he popped.

Cairo tutted and pursed his lips. 'Go on then, share this drastically important news.'

'We. Are. Going. To. The. World. Cup! You, me, McCloud, Ludo, Lightning, Cruncher, Goal Machine and Motorway. We're in the World Cup squad!' he yelled excitedly. Tim paused for Cairo's reaction.

Cairo didn't do anything, apart from look at the baby hedgehog. Tim was expecting a little dance of delight at the very least.

'What about the baby hedgehog?'

'What *about* the baby hedgehog?' asked Tim frustratedly.

'Well, can it come with us? I don't think it's got a mum any more.'

'It's the World Cup, Cairo!' shouted Tim. 'The World Cup! The biggest football competition on the planet. The best countries, the best players, the best managers. Why aren't you more excited? It's what we've always dreamed of.'

'It's what *you've* always dreamed of,' muttered Cairo, holding the baby hedgehog close to his face, inspecting it for fleas. 'Besides, why should I be that bothered about football? After all, I am *rubbish* at it, aren't I?'

Tim couldn't believe it. Why did Cairo have to bring that up again? It was a mistake. He didn't mean to tell Cairo he was rubbish at football. Why didn't Cairo care about the biggest news ever?

'I'm going to tell McCloud!' shouted Tim, stomping out of the room. 'He'll understand how important this is. More important than a stupid baby hedgehog anyway.'

'Some things are more important than football, Tim,' replied Cairo through gritted teeth. 'And the baby hedgehog isn't stupid either. He's very clever.'

Tim slammed the door behind him for full impact. He could feel his blood bubbling away with rage inside him. He couldn't believe Cairo wasn't bothered about the World Cup.

McCloud was sitting outside his caravan lacing up an ancient-looking pair of football boots. Tim bounded up to the Scottish coach.

'You'll never guess what,' he called.

'This better be good, laddie,' growled McCloud. 'I've got an amazing free-kick routine in ma head, and I don't want to be forgetting it.'

'WEAREGOINGTOTHEWORLDCUP,' yelled Tim.

'Eh?'

'WEAREGOINGTOTHEWORLDCUPMCCLOUD.'

McCloud bowed his head and dropped the boot he was lacing up. He went totally silent.

'Did you hear me?' asked Tim. 'You, me, Cairo, four llamas and Motorway are going to the World Cup!'

McCloud's head rose slowly, as though someone was pulling it up on a string. A huge grin was smeared across his face. The widest smile Tim had ever seen him pull. He extended his arms high above his head and then let out the biggest cheer the Gravy farm had ever heard. He then started strutting up and down making trumpet and trombone noises, as well as doing all the actions.

'C'mon, laddie,' bellowed McCloud at the top of his voice. 'Join me!' He grabbed Tim by the shoulder and began marching him up and down outside the caravan, 'Ooom-pa-pa'-ing as he went.

'World Cup! World Cup! World Cup!' they

bellowed, stomping around the training ground. Then the llamas joined them in the parade, marching behind and tossing their heads from side to side. They had no idea what was going on, it just looked like a lot of fun. Then Cruncher did a huge fart and it cleared the training pitch.

An exhausted Tim and McCloud escaped to the safety of the caravan and flopped down on the grass outside. Cairo popped into Tim's head and he remembered their argument.

'Is something up, laddie? You look like you just missed an open goal from a yard out,' asked McCloud, noticing Tim's change of mood.

'We had some really good news, but when I told Cairo he went and ruined it,' said Tim, crossing his arms. 'Sometimes he really doesn't get football.'

McCloud rubbed his chin thoughtfully. Tim and Cairo rarely fell out with each other. Usually it was over what flavour crisps to get at the shop. But this, even to an old stone-heart like McCloud, seemed more important than that.

'D'ye know, that Cairo is one of those strange wee folk who thinks other things are more important than football,' he said in the calmest voice he could muster. 'Apparently for some folks it's quite normal to think other things are more important. Hooses, family, wee bairns, money, food . . . er, love, for example.' McCloud went bright red and did a little shiver when he said 'love'.

'Do you think those things are more important than football, McCloud?' asked Tim.

McCloud let out a loud, deep laugh, which went on a bit too long.

'I live in a caravan, own one tracksuit, dinnae have any money and can tell you who scored every goal for Scotland since 1921. I have devoted ma life to football. It's all I needed. Look what a fine figure of a man I turned out t'be.'

Tim looked down at the wizened old Scotsman, and then realized McCloud wasn't the best person to go to for advice.

'You'll patch it up wi' Cairo,' continued McCloud. 'That's what mates do. Have a wee skirmish and then sort it out that very same day. I dinnae hold grudges – never have, never will.'

'What about the linesman in the Cup final?' asked Tim.

'Ah, OK, maybe nae him.' McCloud scrunched his hands into fists, and a heavy snarl descended on his face.

'Or that Geoff Coren?' said Tim, referring to the Enfield Hotspurts manager who they believe kidnapped Cruncher in the quarter-finals of the Cup. Though they couldn't prove it.

'Hhhmmm, aye, maybe nae him too,' replied McCloud, spitting something on to the ground.

'What about you and Ray Barnowl?'

McCloud shrugged. 'I've nae problem with him,' he said unconvincingly, before quickly moving the subject on. 'Anyway that's beside the point. You and Cairo need to patch it up.'

'Because he's my best friend?'

'No, because he's an excellent llama physio, and he's vital to the team,' said McCloud with a chuckle. Football was much more important than friends to him.

Tim sighed. McCloud was right. Well, half right. Cairo was an excellent physio, but he was also his best friend, and it felt odd being in a bad mood with him. Especially over a baby hedgehog.

LLAMAS NAMED IN ENGLAND SQUAD

By Steve Buffalo-Mozzarella,
Chief Sports Reporter, Daily Megalomaniac

Lightning

Goal Machine

Ludo

Cruncher

The beleaguered England manager Ray Barnowl has sensationally named four llamas in his 23-man/llama squad for this summer's World Cup. Goalkeeper Ludo, winger Lightning, midfielder Cruncher and striker Goal Machine will boost the troubled England team, who struggled during qualification and their recent friendlies.

'I'm delighted to name four llamas from Llama United in my squad for this year's World Cup,' said Ray Barnowl. 'I don't know how they will fit into my starting eleven, but I'm sure I'll work something out. That's why I'm the England manager.'

The decision was greeted warmly by football fans up and down the country, and the protesting crowd that has been camped outside England headquarters for weeks has now dispersed.

Former England striker Ian Wrong was delighted with the squad announcement.

'This is a masterstroke from Barnowl, a genius move. Yesterday everyone hated the geezer, now we all love him. I think England will definitely win the World Cup now.'

The four llamas and their management team of Tim Gravy, McCloud, and Cairo Anderson will join the rest of the England team at their luxury six-star training camp a few days before the tournament begins. The tournament is in the middle of the summer term, and Tim and Cairo aren't allowed to miss too much of school.

'It's going to be an amazing tournament. I'm really hoping the llamas can help England win the World Cup,' said Tim Gravy. 'We've been given some homework to do at the tournament, but c'mon, it's the World Cup – I've got bigger fish to fry. I'm going to leave my homework at home anyway. Don't write that bit down.'

10
WORLD CUP BUILD-UP

Football is an incredibly fickle business. One minute everyone hates you, the next minute you are a hero again. Luckily this rule applied to Ray Barnowl too, and he was back on top of the football pile. Picking the llamas in his World Cup was a masterstroke, even though it wasn't his idea.

He could leave his house without getting booed, and the fruit and veg seller moved his stall to the head offices of the England cricket team.

The tournament was less than two weeks away when a hammer blow was delivered to the competition. The World Cup governing body discovered that the tournament hosts had cheated on their application form and threatened loads of officials to vote for them.

The World Cup had to be moved to another country!

Loads of places that even I've heard of, like Germany, France and Brazil, offered to put on the tournament at the last minute, but in the end an island called Mucho Plata was unusually selected as the host.

Mucho Plata was home to three gazillionaire brothers who had stumbled across large deposits of gold, silver and piles of precious gems while on a walking holiday on the once uninhabited island. I know: how lucky is that? Walking holidays aren't pointless after all! The brothers quickly turned the island into a fabulous tourist destination for the rich and famous. As they were all huge sports fans, they also built some of the most amazing sporting stadiums in the world. All the brothers then had to do was give the football governing body their weight in sweets and a gold rocket car each, and the next thing you know, Mucho Plata was the next World Cup host. What do you mean, there's no such thing as a gold rocket car? There is on Mucho Plata.

Mucho Plata sits in the middle of the Atlantic Ocean, right on the Equator. It is covered in beaches, deserts, jungles and other places that look hot. I've already mentioned how great their stadiums are, but it also has the most amazing hotels, shops, rollercoasters and water slide parks. Oh, and I nearly forgot to tell you that Mucho Plata makes the best chocolate mousse in the world . . . ever. It even has restaurants that *only* serve chocolate mousse!

The change of location didn't bother the players. Like sheep, they just go where they are told. As usual, it was only really annoying to the fans who had to quickly change all their travel plans. But it was such an exciting tournament, they couldn't wait for it to get started, wherever it was.

In their group, England had been drawn against some tough countries: Germany, World Champions so many times I've lost count; Tunisia, one of the best teams in Africa; and Panama, who were a bit of an unknown quantity, which is always dangerous.

Probably one of the toughest World Cups ever, and there certainly wouldn't be any easy games. *Apart from the ones against England*, thought the other countries.

Because Tim and Cairo still had to go to school, they travelled separately from the rest of the England squad, and would arrive just three days before the

Group A

Russia
Saudi Arabia
Egypt
Uruguay

Group B

Portugal
Spain
Morocco
Iran

Group C

France
Australia
Peru
Denmark

Group D

Argentina
Iceland
Croatia
Nigeria

Group E

Brazil
Switzerland
Costa Rica
Serbia

Group F

Belgium
Mexico
Sweden
South Korea

Group G

Germany
Panama
Tunisia
England

Group H

Poland
Senegal
Colombia
Japan

World Cup started. Tim's dad Frank had to come too, because McCloud wasn't considered a responsible adult.

Fiona was furious that she hadn't been invited to the World Cup. In her opinion, her secret visit to Barnowl's office had been crucial in getting the llamas a place in the England squad. Her ninja princess skills were being totally wasted at school. Ninjas do not need to learn long division or what clothes Vikings wore.

The day finally arrived, and the four llamas were placed in the plane's hold in specially designed top-of-the range horseboxes. Cairo was very happy with the llamas' travel arrangements – they were much better than his tiny seat. However, one of the baggage handlers had forgotten to bolt the horseboxes shut. Ten minutes into the flight, Cruncher was first to seize the opportunity for freedom, leaping into the pile of bags at the other end of the hold and taking a huge bite out of a large pink suitcase with a red bow strapped to the handle. Then he ate some swimming trunks, a very posh suit, two pairs of shoes, a toothbrush and nine pairs of pants, all washed down with a large bottle of suncream. Goal Machine was next out of his box and, finding the roundest bag possible, he began booting it around the hold. Then Lightning started practising her sprints and doing the occasional little wee on any blue suitcases she found. She didn't like blue. Ludo remained in his horsebox guarding Motorway. The rest of the plane was far too wild for someone of her importance. She was a princess, after all.

Unaware of the havoc going on beneath him, Tim sat through the flight, worrying that they wouldn't be given enough time to get the llamas to bond with the rest of the England team. Perhaps that's what Ray Barnowl wanted: the llamas wouldn't play properly, and then he wouldn't have to pick them. Tim knew he had done as much llama training as he possibly could. He'd had the White Horse FC players working with them every day and had shown the llamas stacks of video clips of the England players on his mobile phone – though llamas aren't that interested in clips. They tend to dribble on the screen or try and lick it. Cruncher thought it was an ice lolly.

Tim and Cairo's relationship was still a bit frosty from the hedgehog/you're-rubbish-at-football argument, so they didn't sit next to each other on the plane. They were more or less on speaking terms, but it just wasn't as warm as usual. Cairo had spent most of the time back at home nursing the hedgehog, feeding him milk from a little syringe. The hedgehog hadn't come with them to the World Cup. They are a nightmare to get through airport security.

So Tim sat next to McCloud, who spent all his time reading a newspaper. He always started newspapers from the back, where all the sport stories were. He didn't like reading the real news at the front, especially if it involved a celebrity getting married or finding a chocolate bar in her handbag.

Tim glanced absent-mindedly at the back page. Looking down on him was the grinning face of Geoff Coren, the recently sacked manager of Enfield Hotspurts. His hair was as huge as usual, nearly as tall as the man standing next to him in the picture. The other man was broad and

angry-looking, he had a stubbly beard and moustache, a strange blond mullet haircut, and was wearing a pair of goalkeeping gloves.

Tim tried to catch the headline above them as McCloud ruffled the paper up and down.

Core . . . joi . . . many

ren . . . ns . . . Ger

C . . . jo . . . ma . . .

'Will you hold the paper still, McCloud?' asked Tim. 'There's something about Geoff Coren on the back.'

'Aye, I know,' muttered McCloud in reply without looking from the paper.

'What is it?'

'Och, just that he has become the manager of Germany.'

'Germany!'

'Aye, Germany,' replied the unflustered McCloud from behind the paper. 'Funny choice really, the man is a dunderheed. Plus, he cannae speak German.'

'But he used to be a good manager – we had trouble against him. He's won loads of trophies and Germany are one of the best teams in the World Cup.'

'Ppppffftttttt,' replied McCloud dismissively,

ruffling the paper again. 'Nae as good as a team of llamas.'

'But Germany aren't going to play a team of llamas. There are only four of them, and we're not even sure they'll get picked for the matches. We've only got two days to train with the rest of the team.'

'It'll be fine,' muttered McCloud from behind the paper. 'Don't worry, laddie,' he added, not very convincingly.

Tim was still suspicious of McCloud's relationship with Barnowl. There was definitely something funny going on. They must have played professional football around the same time, and Barnowl clearly hated McCloud. Maybe that was why he'd been so reluctant to pick the llamas . . .

'What's the problem with you and Ray Barnowl?' asked Tim.

'Nae idea, hardly know the man,' replied McCloud, without looking out from behind his paper.

'Didn't you play with him?'

McCloud ruffled the paper angrily. 'I played with lots of people – five hundred and sixty-seven league appearances and ninety-eight international caps. I cannae remember everyone.'

Tim stayed quiet for a few seconds. McCloud's

emotional brick wall was back up, and Tim wasn't going to be able to break it down. Then he tapped the back page of the paper again.

'Now what?' barked McCloud, scrunching the paper down and looking Tim directly in the eye.

'Who is this guy next to Coren?' Tim asked as cheerfully as he could, pointing at the photograph.

'Oh, him. Cannae you tell?' replied McCloud, his voice calming when he realized it wasn't another question about Ray Barnowl. 'It's Karl-Heinz Torstooper. He's had a wee haircut, and it looks like he is trying to smile. So he looks slightly different.'

'Torstooper,' cooed Tim in admiration. 'The greatest goalkeeper in the world?'

'That's right, laddie, now he *is* a tricky biggen. We'll have to go some to get past him. He started his career in England when he was much younger, but went back to Germany and became the greatest keeper ever. They call him the Golden Octopus. What a player.' McCloud looked up at the ceiling as though he was trying to hold back a tear. 'They dinnae make them like that any more.'

'Have you heard of the Golden Octopus, Cairo?' Tim called across the seats, trying to engage his friend in some sort of friendly conversation.

Cairo shrugged and looked away, turning to talk to Frank. He didn't care about the Golden Octopus. He was missing his hedgehog.

11
MEET THE ENGLAND TEAM

The rest of the England team were already well settled into the six-star training facility, hotel and spa resort when the weary travellers arrived in a super-fancy black car and llama trailer. The journey from the airport had taken over six hours and everyone was totally exhausted. They were hungry, thirsty and had boiling hot bottoms from the car's seat warmers.

It hadn't been much fun for the llamas in the small trailer. Well, not as much fun as the flight. Cairo had told them off about the mess they had made in the hold of the plane, but they didn't really know what he was talking about. In the trailer Cruncher ate most of the upholstery and chewed both door handles, Lightning and Goal Machine's coats were disheveled, and Motorway was clearly angry about the shamefully unroyal conditions she had been left in. Only Ludo seemed unflustered by the trip, staying calm and solid throughout.

Cairo's mood hadn't improved by the time he arrived at the hotel, and he shouted at the driver and the staff at the hotel for the poor llama transport until the hotel manager escorted them to some top-notch stables at the back of the hotel, which seemed to calm Cairo down a little. The four llamas, however, seemed quite upset, even after they were given some fresh grass and water and somewhere to have a nice sit-down. Ludo took up a place by the fence and began looking down the road, as though he was waiting for someone or something to appear.

After a tedious twenty-minute wait in the hotel lobby, Tim and McCloud were finally greeted by the England assistant manager, Nigel Yes, a forgettable man with a . . . erm . . . oh, I've forgotten. Ignoring McCloud, he ushered Tim through the magnificent marble hotel reception and outside to the huge pool arca. McCloud followed behind, making sure he zipped his tracksuit right up under his chin, even though the sun was melting everything in sight.

He was greeted by an awesome sight. The whole England team were lounging around the pool soaking up the sun. There were piles of drinks, fruit and sweets stacked around them, and lots of people massaging their expensive footballers' legs. Even though he'd met loads of footballers already, Tim still felt a hot tingle of excitement shoot up his back.

There was the huge Loverpoo centre-back, Sid Melonhead, about to dive into the pool; Nork Town's star midfielder Jim Hoisin was throwing bits of cake in the air and catching them in his mouth; full-back Steve Crispy was trying to trim his nostril hair; and T. J. Wilkinson was reading a book . . . the right way round!

'Everyone, this is Tim Gravy,' announced Nigel Yes to the group, 'and an old Scotsman.'

McCloud nodded his head slightly at the players and then slunk off towards a juice bar just inside the hotel. He wasn't impressed with meeting footballers.

'Hi,' squeaked Tim, lifting his hand to give a little self-conscious wave.

A handful of players looked up from what they were doing, but only T. J. Wilkinson was nice enough to wave back.

Tim felt his heart sink into his trainers. He hadn't thought about how he and the llamas would be received by the players. After all, some of them would lose their places in the team to the four-legged stars.

A hairy face suddenly popped up through a gap in the sun-loungers and began chewing on one of the players' towels. It was Cruncher, and it was clearly a very tasty towel.

There was a huge splash as Lightning bounced off the diving board head first into the pool, sending the England players scrambling for cover. She swam a few lengths, got out and shook her coat all over some of the cowering England stars.

Then a hail of oranges flew towards the hotel doors, causing Tim to duck out of the way. It was Goal Machine skilfully volleying

a bowl of fruit he had found. He was now eyeing a massive watermelon.

'No, Goal Machine,' Tim warned, but it was too late.

Goal Machine nudged the watermelon out of the bowl, chipped it up into the air and then smashed it as hard as he could towards the hotel. It exploded immediately on impact with his foot, showering the players around him with thick sticky lumps of red watermelon and black pips. Goal Machine didn't get a bit on him.

Cairo skidded into the pool area and began frantically rounding up the three llamas.

'Hey, I thought you were supposed to be looking after them,' said Tim, scolding his friend.

Cairo gave Tim a withering glance. 'I was checking on Ludo. He seems really upset,' he said through gritted teeth. 'I turned my back for two seconds and these three wandered off. They're your responsibility too, you know. But you are too busy with your . . . *new friends*, aren't you?'

Cairo got hold of the llamas and led them away. Cruncher grabbed another towel as a tasty pudding on the way out.

The England players turned and stared at Tim.

He felt about two inches tall. How embarrassing. A row with his best friend, and his llamas seemingly out of control, in front of all these famous footballers.

'Perhaps we'd better go and meet the captain. This is a bit awkward, isn't it?' said Nigel Yes, whispering behind his hand.

Tim nodded in agreement. McCloud reappeared at his shoulder holding a huge pink-and-green cocktail with a banana floating in it. Nigel Yes gave him and the banana a sneer.

'We should meet the England manager, too. Can't forget him, can we?' added Nigel Yes. 'You can stay out here, McCloud. We don't need you.'

12
GREG PUNCH

Nigel Yes led Tim into a large games room at the side of the hotel, full of pool tables, ping-pong tables, dartboards and video games. There was also a disco, a bar, and a chef, who was serving a huge burger with double cheese, bacon and curly fries to a large defender called Preston Cheeks. *Not very healthy for a professional footballer*, thought Tim.

In a dark corner of the games room, two men were playing an intense game of cards. This wasn't Snap. Both had two huge piles of cash next to them and they looked annoyed at being disturbed. Standing uncomfortably next to them was Ray Barnowl.

'Greg Punch, Jack Chilly and Mr Ray Barnowl, of course,' said Nigel Yes, wafting a limp hand at the trio. He then turned and melted away into the background. The larger of the two card players stood up and shook Tim's hand. It was so powerful and crushing, Tim squeaked with pain. The man seemed to enjoy this.

'I'm Greg Punch, England captain and midfielder. People call me the engine room of the team,' boomed Punch. He was enormous, with a thick neck, short-shaved haircut and sleeves of tattoos up both arms. Tim had seen him in action many times and was not a fan of his playing style. Neither was McCloud.

'He's a dunderheed goon,' the Scottish coach would say. 'He has nae skill with the fitba' at his feet, so he uses his muscles to get by. He ruins matches by bashin' people up. He'd be better off on a rugby pitch.'

Tim couldn't understand why Greg Punch was England captain, or even in the team. He just wasn't that good.

Jack Chilly remained seated. He was a lazy man, but had the amazing skill of being in the right place at the right time and had been England's top scorer for the past five years. Tim had never seen Chilly sprint or challenge for a header, he just seemed to amble about the pitch as though he owned the place.

Chilly nodded to Tim and returned to studying his cards.

'So you think your llamas are going to improve my

England team?' asked Punch with a chuckle.

'That's the plan, I hope,' replied Tim, casting a glance at Barnowl for some moral support. Barnowl's face was unmoved. If anything, he looked a little scared.

'Well, look here, little boy,' said Punch with a grimace, looming in closer on Tim's face. 'We've got a settled team here. We qualified for the World Cup without your flaming llamas, so I can't see them getting in the team.' He glared at Barnowl. 'Especially in the positions they play. We're already really strong in those areas.'

Tim felt a bead of sweat trickle down his back. His throat had gone incredibly dry. Cairo would be good in this situation, he thought. He'd be able to say something witty in reply to Punch's aggressive comments.

'Erm, I suppose that's up to the manager,' said Tim with a weedy squeak. He looked at Barnowl for support again, but nothing was coming back. The manager seemed hypnotized by Greg Punch.

'I'm surprised they even got picked. That's media pressure for you, I suppose.' Punch shot a withering look at Barnowl, who visibly shrivelled, hunching his shoulders and bowing his head as though he had just been told off for forgetting his homework.

'You'd best be off and check on your llamas, hadn't you, little boy?' continued Punch as he sat back down and starting moving his large pile of money.

Tim edged his way away from the men and back out into the bright sunshine of the poolside. He felt utterly crushed and empty inside. Meeting the England squad for the first time was not the experience he had expected. He was here to help England win the World Cup. They should have been happy to see him and the llamas.

McCloud appeared at Tim's shoulder. His tracksuit was still zipped right up to his neck and his flat cap was firmly fixed to his head. Tim felt even hotter just looking at him.

'So,' he said with a large sigh. 'Lemme guess. That was an awful wee tour of the squad.'

'How did you know?' said Tim.

'They're footballers,' replied McCloud. 'You get some good 'uns and you get some bad 'uns. I have a feelin' this team has quite a few bad 'uns. Like when one tangerine in a crate goes mouldy, the rest turn bad overnight.'

Tim wasn't really sure what McCloud was getting at.

'What about you, McCloud? Are you a nice one or a horrible one?' said Tim.

McCloud laughed and then gave a small shrug. 'I'm neither. I'm just a legend.'

13
GRUMPY LLAMAS

The start of the World Cup was only two days away, and Tim and McCloud were keen to get in as much training as they could before the opening match against their biggest rivals, Germany. The draw had been unkind to England, but at least they would get their toughest opposition out of the way early.

Barnowl suggested that the llamas trained away from the England team until they got used to the facilities. Tim wasn't keen on this idea, but he had found the England team so unwelcoming, and Punch particularly unpleasant, that he didn't really kick up a fuss. The llamas were probably best kept away from them, for now.

Cairo led Goal Machine, Lightning and Cruncher to the training pitch on the far side of the hotel. All of them had their heads bowed, including Cairo.

'What's up?' said Tim, placing some training cones carefully around the pitch. 'You all look totally miserable.'

Cairo shrugged. He clearly wasn't in the mood to talk.

'Hang on,' said Tim. 'Where's Ludo?'

'He wouldn't come,' replied Cairo flatly. 'So Motorway wouldn't come either.'

'What do you mean, Ludo wouldn't come?'

'Exactly what I said. He wouldn't come.'

'He doesn't have a choice, Cairo,' said Tim, his voice beginning to rise slightly. 'He's a professional footballer who is going to be playing in the World Cup.'

Cairo rolled his eyes. 'He's not a professional footballer,' he said with a sigh. 'He's a llama who happens to be very good at football.'

'He does football for a job,' said Tim, folding his arms and grinding his teeth together. 'That makes him a professional. So where is he?'

Cairo took a deep breath and shut his eyes, trying to control his own temper. He didn't want to shout at Tim, but it seemed to be getting harder every day.

'I tried to get Ludo to come, but he wants to stay

close to the fence so he can look down the road. I've not seen him like this since we first got him,' said Cairo.

'What do you think is up?'

'Dunno, homesick maybe. We are a long way from the farm. Although he wasn't like this when we did all the touring.'

'PEEEEEEEEPPPPPPP,' said McCloud's whistle, making Tim and Cairo jump out of their skin.

'C'mon, boys,' shouted the Scottish coach. 'We dinnae have time for this mucking about. We've got to get this lot ready for the match. We can deal with Ludo later.'

Tim nodded, and emptied some training balls from the kitbag on to the pitch, then he noticed something glinting on top of one of the llamas.

Perched on top of Lightning's head was a very expensive pair of large circular-shaped sunglasses. The gold pattern on the rims and arms sparkled in the midday sun.

'I have absolutely no idea where those came from,' said Cairo. 'Better get them off her, she can't play in those.'

He made a grab for the glasses, but Lightning

was too quick and ducked underneath his hand. She wasn't very happy with Cairo's attempt to mess with her fashion statement and gave him a very stern look. Cairo backed away.

'Let's leave that little problem too,' he said.

Training did not go well. The llamas were totally uninterested in playing football. They were all in foul moods. 'Foul' moods, geddit? No? OK, I'll move on.

Cruncher spotted a pile of grounds equipment by the side of the pitch and occasionally wandered off to take sly little nibbles of the wheelbarrow or a drink of the pitch paint, which to a llama tastes like coconut water. Lightning kept her scowling face on for all of training and couldn't be bothered to run for any balls. Running fast was her best skill, but today even McCloud could comfortably jog past her, and slugs were usually faster than him. Goal Machine's performance was the most worrying. All his shots and headers at goal were missing the target by miles. He looked clumsy and out of form – what McCloud called a severe case of the 'weebee jeebies'. Anyone else would call it 'being rubbish'.

'What's up with them, Cairo?' Tim demanded as they tidied up after training. McCloud had already gone back to the hotel 'to put some ice down his pants', as he was finally feeling the Mucho Plata heat.

'How should I know?' replied Cairo, his voice crackling with anger.

'You're the team physio, you *should* know!' barked Tim.

'I can keep them fit and healthy. It doesn't mean I know what's going on inside their heads.'

Tim and Cairo were really close to each other now, you could feel the heat from their argument bouncing off them.

'You're not looking after them properly,' shouted Tim, angrily waving his fist in the air.

Cairo inwardly fumed, screwing and unscrewing his fists.

'Never accuse me of not looking after animals properly,' he hissed through gritted teeth. He turned on his heels and stormed away.

Tim watched his friend stomp off with the llamas trailing behind. He wasn't really sure what to do, his face was burning hot and his heart was leaping around like a jack-in-the-box. Hearing someone laughing in the distance, he looked back towards the hotel and saw Greg Punch standing on the wall that overlooked the training pitch.

'Not looking good for you, little boy!' he bellowed with a cackle. 'Training-ground bust-up, and now I'm afraid I've got some more bad news.'

'Oh yeah?' replied Tim, trying his hardest not to be scared by the England captain. 'What's that, then?'

'Starting line-up has already been picked for the match on Saturday,' said Punch gleefully. 'Your llamas aren't in it.'

From being boiling hot with rage, Tim suddenly went as cold as a packet of garden peas that had been left at the back of a freezer. He knew there had been something fishy about being told to train away from the rest of the England team. He should have realized they weren't going to get picked for the first match. He cursed himself for being so foolish.

'I told you they'd have no chance getting into a settled team,' continued Punch. 'We don't need llamas in the England squad. They are best on the bench . . . or better still, on a flight back home.'

Punch laughed loudly again, turned and hopped off the wall, wandering back into the group of training England players. He gave Barnowl a big slap on the back. It didn't look like a particularly friendly one, and Barnowl didn't greet him with a smile. What was going on between those two?

Tim was on his own in the middle of the training pitch. He felt like he didn't have a friend in the world.

14
THE GOLDEN OCTOPUS

Karl-Heinz Torstooper sat in the German training room, half an hour before the opening World Cup match with England. The Golden Octopus was taking deep lungfuls of air. After over 200 games in the German number one jersey, this would be his last tournament, and he wanted to take it all in. The man was an absolute legend in his home country. Everyone thought he was brilliant, even the German clubs he didn't play for. Boys and girls, men and women, wore lovely little Golden Octopus badges and would take huge Golden Octopus flags to matches to wave.

Outside of Germany everyone knew he was great, but he wasn't as popular because he had crushed the footballing dreams of Brazil, Argentina, Holland, France, Spain, Italy and many other international and club teams with his goalkeeping talent. He saved last-minute penalties, blocked one-on-ones and pulled off stunning fingertip saves. Goalkeepers are rarely given the credit for a team's success, but Torstooper had always been a driving force.

He had started his career in England as a fairly average goalkeeper, but after returning to Germany, now more than twelve years ago, he very quickly went from average to magnificent, as though he had been struck by a bolt of brilliance from the footballing gods. These new-found skills made him a bit pompous, and he started to talk a bit like an emperor.

'Torstooper is the greatest footballer alive or dead,' is something he might say, or, 'Torstooper would like a cheese-and-pickle sandwich,' or, 'Torstooper would like to return this cheese-and-pickle sandwich because it is a cheese Torstooper does not like. Torstooper only eats cheese with holes in it.'

When he was being *really* pompous, he would call himself the 'Golden Octopus'. For example, 'The Golden Octopus is going to go to the toilet. There had better be the correct paper available.'

Torstooper was usually followed around by a strange bearded man in a straw boater hat called Heinrich Prussia. This was Torstooper's agent. He would just hang around Torstooper telling him how great he was and how terrible everyone else was. He was annoying and not particularly pleasant, like a verruca that won't go away. Torstooper, however, couldn't live without him. It was Prussia who had helped make him the player he was now, all those years ago.

'You'd better go out and warm up,' said Prussia, bustling into the changing room as though he had frogs in his pants. 'Where is that idiot of a new manager, Coren? An Englishman managing the German team, it's a disgrace! This wouldn't have happened in my playing days.'

'Torstooper quite likes him,' said Torstooper. 'He will help us win the World Cup.'

'*You* will win the World Cup, Karl-Heinz,' said Prussia. 'Not a small Englishman with large hair. It is you that owns this team. Without you, Germany is nothing.' He smashed his walking stick against the door to show he meant business.

Torstooper removed his tracksuit bottoms and began jumping up and down to warm up before he went outside.

'Look at those strong legs,' said Prussia, in admiration. 'Legendary legs – nobody has legs like these. Raw power, made of solid German iron.'

Torstooper smiled and began catching imaginary footballs.

'This English team is useless,' continued Prussia. 'I have already told their manager this in the tunnel. I've also been on TV this morning to tell the world that England is rubbish.'

'Torstooper is going outside now,' said Torstooper, and he marched out into the tunnel.

He bumped straight into Cairo as he came through the door. Cairo was carrying two heavy bags full of water bottles, which he was taking to the llamas back in their transporter. They scattered all over the floor and began rolling away. Cairo bent down to pick them up as Torstooper stood over him.

'You are in the way of Torstooper,' he said firmly.

'Jeez, I'm just trying to pick up all these bottles, hold your horses,' muttered Cairo.

'You are still in the way of Torstooper,' repeated the German keeper.

'OK, OK,' said Cairo hastily, dropping bottles back into the bags. He looked up at the goalkeeper who was standing above him like a colossus. Something looked very familiar. He racked his brain. Where had he seen those legs before?

'Torstooper will be stepping over you now,' said

the keeper. 'You are taking too long for Torstooper.' And with that he strode off down the tunnel.

'I'm really starting to hate football,' muttered Cairo to himself under his breath. 'The sooner this tournament ends, the better. It's turning everyone mad.'

15
GERMANY V ENGLAND

Tim's worry that Germany would be too strong for England without the llamas came true almost instantly. Germany cut through England's defence like a hot knife through butter. It was 2 – 0 after just fifteen minutes.

Not that Tim could see who actually scored the goals – he had a terrible view. As a member of the England coaching staff, he was given a seat in the dugout, but it was behind all the rest of the coaching staff and all the substitutes, on the very back row. So he was constantly having to shift around in his seat to see between all the heads sitting in front of him. Poor McCloud had been given a seat at the very back row on the other side of the stadium. As far away as possible from the England dugout. Apparently it was the only free seat available. Which we all know was a lie.

Craning his neck, Tim saw England striker Jack Chilly strolling around with his hands on his hips, and the captain, Greg Punch, clattering everything that moved, including his own players. Tim knew McCloud would be fuming about the defence and would probably be calling them dunderheads. Cairo wasn't much help either. With no llamas on the pitch, his interest in the game was minimal. He spent most of the game staring at the German side of the pitch and seemed very interested in the Golden Octopus. Tim had to agree that watching Torstooper patrol his area like a caged tiger was a lot more interesting than watching England blunder about the pitch.

It was 3 – 0 at half-time and the changing room was so full of people, Tim could only just about squeeze in. Coaches, players, physios, doctors, osteopaths (whatever they are) and a man selling watermelons took up every inch of space. What he didn't hear was anyone shouting, as he had expected. If it had been McCloud in charge instead of Barnowl, he would be so angry his voice would be tearing paint off the walls. All he could hear was the soft hubbub of people muttering to each other and the chinking of tea cups. Where was the passion? This was the World Cup!

Barnowl inched himself into the room and began

clearing his throat so that everyone would stop what they were doing and listen to him. This took ages, mainly because everyone seemed to be arguing about who had the knife to cut up the watermelons.

Ah, thought Tim. *Here comes the big uplifting speech that will stir the team into a momentous comeback win.*

'So then,' said Barnowl meekly. 'This is not going as well as I expected. I think we need to try a little bit harder in the second half. Maybe get a shot or two on the German goal. We haven't really tested their keeper much, and I think he could be a bit dodgy.'

Tim shook his head in disbelief. One word you couldn't use to describe Torstooper was 'dodgy'.

'Let's just do them,' roared Punch, smashing his fist on the physio table in the middle of the room. The rest of the team cheered their approval. Then went back to discussing the watermelon.

Punch's team talk was slightly better than Barnowl's, thought Tim, but it was hardly a tactical masterclass.

In the fifty-sixth minute of the match, England had their first shot on the German goal. T. J. Wilkinson, the only England player who appeared to be having a good game, charged down the right wing and zipped in a lethal low cross, cutting the German defence in half. Jack Chilly strolled casually into the area and poked the ball towards the gaping net. He raised his arms in celebration and waited for the back of the net to bulge.

Germany 3 – 1 England . . .

Oh, hang on, what was this? The outstretched boot of the Golden Octopus, in mid-splits as he flew across the goal, tipped it away. Tim spat his high-energy drink out all over the seat in front of him. He had never seen anything like it. The save of the century!

The German team mobbed their super-keeper to congratulate him, but he wasn't interested. He was already focused on his next job, dealing with the England corner, which Dwain Drain kicked straight out. The best save and the worst corner ever in the space of a minute. That's football.

Tim looked across at the German dugout. There sat their manager, Geoff Coren, the man he suspected had kidnapped Cruncher in the Cup last season. Coren looked very pleased with himself and his new team. He'd hardly moved all game and just seemed to be enjoying the match. Why wouldn't he? Germany were 3 – 0 up and coasting to victory.

Coren caught Tim's gaze and held it for what seemed like ages, smiling smugly. Tim and Llama United had got the better of him in an epic Cup match last season, but now the boot was on the other foot. Tim felt uncomfortable. Here was a man in total control of his amazing team, while Tim felt like a helpless, unwelcome hanger-on.

Coren broke his gaze to see Germany roll in their fourth goal of the match. There would be tougher teams to get stressed about later in the tournament. He knew England wouldn't be one of them. They'd be lucky to get to the second round.

After the game, Tim and Cairo went to check on the llamas and Motorway, who had been left in a transporter outside the stand for the whole match. Technically, they could have been used as substitutes, but Tim knew they weren't going to be given a game. What was Barnowl playing at?

The llamas looked incredibly grumpy. They were usually pleased to see Tim and Cairo, but they could hardly be bothered to lift their heads. Tim attempted to stroke Ludo under his chin. He loved being tickled there, but today he wasn't bothered. He even moved his head away.

Cairo busied himself topping up their water and food. He spent a lot of time thinking about why the llamas were so grumpy, but was worried that bringing the subject up again would cause another argument. He was still in a big huff about the argument the other day, and wasn't in the mood to talk to Tim unless he heard an apology.

'That German keeper is amazing,' said Tim, trying to start a conversation. He didn't like Cairo being so quiet. 'Not as good as our Ludo, though.' Tim gave Ludo a rub on the nose, which he didn't seem to enjoy.

Cairo secretly rolled his eyes. He still hadn't heard an apology yet.

'Torstooper used to live in England, you know,' said Tim, babbling on. 'When he was a lot younger.

He played for a team that is quite close to where we live. But they let him go on a free transfer and he moved back to Germany. Biggest mistake ever – now he's the greatest keeper in the world.'

Cairo didn't care if the German keeper had lived next door, and after their meeting in the tunnel he hoped he'd never see him again. Although something was troubling him about the man . . . Those legs did look familiar. Now Tim was chatting as though nothing had happened yesterday, and it was making him angrier.

Lightning started stamping her feet up and down and making tutting noises.

'What's up with her?' asked Tim.

Cairo went over to the winger and tried to calm her down with a soothing humming noise.

'I think I've worked it out,' said Cairo breaking his silence. 'But I don't want to tell you until you say sorry.'

'Sorry for what?' exclaimed Tim.

Cairo tutted and shook his head in frustration.

'Sorry for what?!' repeated Tim, his voice getting louder.

Cairo whacked his bucket down on the floor and stormed out of the transporter, slamming the door

behind him. Tim couldn't believe Cairo was being so sensitive, and he clearly wasn't concentrating on their World Cup mission. What was wrong with everyone?

Before he had time to think that question over, the trailer suddenly filled with the most horrific smell you could imagine. As though someone had mixed broccoli, sprouts, baked beans and cabbage into one huge, smelly smoothie.

Tim looked at the llamas. Cruncher had a nasty scowl on his face and one of his legs sticking out at a right angle. As though he had every intention of delivering a knockout blow.

'Oh no, Cruncher, please no . . . not again,' Tim called to the midfielder. It was too late.

PPPPPRRRRRRRPPPPAAARRRRPPPPPP.

16
THE HOTEL LOBBY FRACAS

Things didn't get much better for England and the llamas in their second match of the tournament. A 0 – 0 draw with Tunisia, the most boring match in the history of football. Even I'm falling asleep thinking about it.

Once again, Barnowl didn't pick the llamas. This made the England fans furious. They hadn't travelled all this way for a 0 – 0 draw and no llamas. Now England had to beat Panama in the next game and hope that Tunisia would lose to Germany, otherwise they had no chance. England needed a miracle.

Tim, Cairo and the rest of the England squad returned to the six-star hotel a few hours after the game. McCloud was waiting for them in the hotel lobby. It looked like he was on the verge of a meltdown, and not because he seemed to be wearing two thick football training jackets in forty-degree heat. McCloud's face was as purple as Scottish heather, probably not the colour a face should be. His lips were pursed so tightly they'd gone white, and he was pacing up and down, arms folded across his chest. A furious type of pacing, quick and menacing, as though he was a cheetah waiting for his dinner.

McCloud was waiting for Barnowl.

'BARNOWL,' he yelled at the top of his voice as soon as Barnowl had placed one foot inside the hotel lobby. Everyone in the room stopped what they were doing straight away. The receptionist cut short her phone gabbling, the bellboy knocked over three suitcases, the doorman let go of the door he was holding open for a very rich family, hotel guests stopped drinking their tea, and the watermelon seller dropped one on his foot. Do you think he is following us around?

'BARNOWL!' McCloud stormed across the lobby and grabbed the England manager by the lapels of his expensive suit. McCloud was a lot stronger than he looked and managed to lift Barnowl a few inches off the floor. Their faces were so close their noses touched, and McCloud's shouting became a furious hiss.

'I came to this World Cup to train the llamas and help you win it,' he said. 'But you've got me goin' on pointless scouting trips and you've nae even let the llamas on the pitch. Look at the team, it's a pile of goons. Panama will batter you unless you pull it together and let our llamas have a go out there.'

Greg Punch and the goalkeeper Pete Badger appeared behind Barnowl, the two toughest players on the England team. The colour instantly returned to Barnowl's cheeks. In fact he looked very composed considering his feet weren't touching the floor.

'Think you'd better be putting Barnowl back on the floor,' said Greg Punch, leaning close in to McCloud. Pete Badger cracked his knuckles menacingly.

McCloud ignored the request. He wasn't scared of Greg Punch, even if everyone else was. He lifted

Barnowl up a tiny bit more, although it was starting to hurt his wrists.

'For the mighty JTs, you cannae ignore me, Barnowl,' hissed McCloud. 'I led a team of llamas to the Cup final, I scored the winner against West Germany. I have more medals and international caps than you have had hot dinners. Me and the boys are here to save the England team from international oblivion. START PICKING THE LLAMAS. THE WHOLE COUNTRY WANTS THEM ON THE PITCH.'

'That's not going to happen while I'm around,' said Greg Punch. He signalled to Pete Badger and the duo swiftly removed McCloud's hands from Barnowl's jacket, and the England manager's feet dropped to the floor. Punch and Badger grabbed McCloud and in the blink of an eye had secured him tightly to the hotel lobby floor by sitting on him.

'I think we've had enough from you, McCloud,' said Punch calmly into McCloud's ear.

'I didn't want you in the coaching team,' said Barnowl, readjusting his suit and leaning down to face the immobile McCloud. 'However, the boy was so insistent that we had to accept it.'

'HHMMMMPPPFFFQQTTHHHHSSS,'

mumbled McCloud into Badger's armpit.

'I HATE YOU, MCCLOUD,' Barnowl continued with a snarl. 'My bad knee is a permanent reminder of what you did to me all those years ago at Badison Park. Remember?'

Punch lifted his knuckles off McCloud's cheek so he could reply.

'What yer talkin aboot . . . ?'

'Typical! You don't even remember what you did. You were so full of yourself, you didn't notice other players like me trying to earn a living and play the game we loved.'

'I cannae remember every game I played. It was over five hoondred matches!'

'Well, I can. I only played ten matches, before a wild Scottish midfielder did a two-footed tackle on my knee . . . and shattered it into a million pieces.' Barnowl's voice began to tremble and he wiped a small tear out of the corner of his eye.

McCloud remained silent. His face had changed from one of anger to one of shame. For the first time ever, Tim felt sorry for Barnowl. His career had been cut short by McCloud. The coach he had grown to admire over the last year or so was nothing more than a footballing thug and no better than Greg Punch.

101

Tim felt like someone had two–footed–tackled him in the stomach.

'Now get this man out of my sight,' said Barnowl. 'Don't go near my team. It is over.'

McCloud didn't put up a struggle as Punch and Badger gleefully marched him out of the hotel lobby. Tim glanced across at Cairo, who looked totally stunned. This wouldn't improve his opinion of football, and it was already at an all–time low.

Cairo threw up his hands and marched off towards his room without saying a word.

17
LISTENING LUDO

Tim was in a daze as he left the hotel lobby and wandered out past the pool and towards the training pitches. His brain couldn't compute what had happened since they'd arrived in Mucho Plata. Everything that could have gone wrong, had gone wrong.

The llamas were as grumpy as Tim had ever seen them; Cairo was in a really bad mood and seemed to have completely lost interest in the World Cup campaign; the England team were still rubbish; and now McCloud had been exposed as someone who had ruined another player's career. The only person who seemed to be enjoying himself was Tim's dad, Frank. He had been lazing around, sunbathing, drinking cocktails and reading lots of books. He looked genuinely relaxed for the first time in ages.

After about five minutes of aimless wandering,

Tim found himself beside the luxury stables where Ludo, Lightning, Goal Machine, Cruncher and Motorway were staying. Ludo was still close to the fence, staring down the road. Lightning, who was usually constantly roaming around, was sitting in the middle of the field, not moving. Cruncher was standing by a huge trough of fresh food that he hadn't touched. At least Goal Machine was near a football, though he missed every time he tried to kick it.

'Oh, Ludo,' said Tim with a big sigh. 'Everything is rubbish.' His chin sank down on to his chest and he blew out a slow puff of air.

Ludo glanced at Tim briefly, before returning to his staring-down-the-road duties.

'Why is everyone is so miserable?' Tim asked. 'The World Cup should be the happiest time of our lives, but we are all wandering around with faces like slapped bottoms. Picking you guys in the team would make everything better, wouldn't it?'

Ludo didn't respond.

'What's down that road, Ludo?' asked Tim.

Ludo sniffed, but didn't turn his head.

'I think he's missing everyone,' came a familiar voice from the other side of the large stable. It was Frank.

He appeared clutching a large bright yellow cocktail with a tiny green umbrella in it. He was wearing blue swimming shorts and a pair of sunglasses that he'd pinched from Beetroot before he came on holiday – sorry, I mean 'to the serious World Cup tournament'. His skin was a terrible shade of pink.

'Dad! What are you doing round here?' asked Tim.

'Oh, I always come here before the sun goes down, to get away from the idiot England team around the pool,' Frank replied. 'It's quiet and I can read my book.' He waved a copy of *Dads: How Not to Be a Fool* in the air. 'Sounds like you're having a bit of trouble,' he continued kindly.

Tim nodded, rubbing his left eye. Everything was getting on top of him and he could feel some tears bubbling up behind his nose. He didn't want to cry. He was supposed to be a tough football coach.

'It's all right to feel like this,' said Frank. 'Being a manager of anything can be really tough; everyone expects you to make all the right decisions.'

Tim sniffed and rubbed his eye again. For the first time in ages, Ludo turned his head to look at him. The big, strong llama looked concerned.

'Do you want a hug?' said Frank.

Tim nodded and threw himself into the open arms of his dad.

Frank made an uncomfortable 'Gggrrrrrrr' noise under his breath as Tim's arms wrapped around his sunburned body. But he didn't let on it was painful, he just dealt with it. His book had taught him that.

'I hope you don't mind,' said Frank after a few seconds of hugging, 'but I've done something that might help with some of the problems you've got.'

'Oh, what's that?' asked Tim.

'I called Cairo's mum and told her to bring the rest of the llamas over here.'

'ALL the llamas!!! Why?'

'I sort of overheard Cairo and McCloud talking the other day. Cairo thinks these guys are missing the other llamas at home. They need to be together, as a team. Splitting them up has caused this problem. Once they are back together, he reckoned they'd all start playing well again.'

'Really?' said Tim, not believing what his dad was saying. 'All the llamas, coming over here?'

'Yep. McCloud was going to sort it out, but I noticed he was in such a bad mood today, I thought I'd step in and help. I'm hardly busy here after all.'

Tim gave Ludo a big cheerful pat on his back. 'So that's why you've been looking down the road all this time,' he said. 'They'll be here soon, Ludo. Everything will be better.'

Just as Tim was about to give Ludo a tickle under his chin, a dark thought entered his head. Why hadn't Cairo told him about this problem sooner? Why had he just told McCloud? They were supposed to be best friends, so why wasn't he talking to him?

18
THE EVIL MAYONNAISE

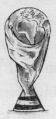

The next day a loud, high-pitched scream came from the poolside. This wasn't uncommon, as some members of the England team were prone to pranks. Silly stuff like splatting cake in each other's faces, cutting up someone's pants and stuffing gherkins up people's noses when they were sleeping. They were supposed to be grown men!

This scream was slightly different, though, and brought with it a flood of doctors and physios, and eventually an ambulance. Even Lightning popped over for a look through the fence, but she was shooed away by one of the players.

The lazy England striker Jack Chilly had knocked a jar of mayonnaise on to his foot, trying to dunk a chip directly into it. I know – how unhygienic! Especially as Chilly was a well-known double-dipper. The jar was one of those big, heavy ones, and it knew nothing about expensive footballers' feet, promptly breaking three of Jack Chilly's metatarsals. For those of us who are not doctors, these are the toe bones. All I know is that it hurts, and England's top scorer was out of the World Cup! Tim would have kissed the jar of mayonnaise, if it hadn't broken into ten pieces when it thundered into Chilly's foot.

The England squad was packed with defensive players and only had three strikers: Chilly, Jo Hussain-Bolt and Goal Machine. Chilly wouldn't play again for months, so that left Hussain-Bolt and Goal Machine to vie for the empty striker's jersey. Tim knew that Hussain-Bolt would be the obvious choice to step in for Chilly. The llamas were at the bottom of Barnowl's pecking order. However, with one less player in his way, Goal Machine's chances of playing were much higher, even if his bad mood had made him rubbish at football.

With the prospect of the rest of his family and the llamas flying in to offer their support, Tim was feeling brave. So, later that evening, in the grand hotel dining room, Tim approached Barnowl as he was tucking into a large chocolate mousse – the speciality of Mucho Plata, if you remember.

'What is it now?' asked Barnowl snappily.

He knew Tim would be asking about the llamas being picked for the final group game with Panama. He was totally fed up with being asked about the llamas. The media had been on his back about it all afternoon, during a boring three-hour press conference, especially now that Jack Chilly was injured.

'We've got to beat Panama in the game tomorrow, or we are out,' said Tim. 'A draw isn't enough with such a rubbish goal difference.'

'Well, durrr,' replied Barnowl scornfully. 'Don't you think I know that already? I *am* the manager.'

'You need to pick Goal Machine to replace Chilly, or Lightning to cross the ball in for Hussain-Bolt. You also need to pick Cruncher and Ludo.'

Greg Punch slid into the seat next to Barnowl like a big thick slug. *What was he doing here?* Punch had a false fixed grin on his face that made him appear even more mean and threatening.

'Any problems here, boss?' he asked through his false smile. He stuck his finger straight in Barnowl's chocolate mousse, scooped a large dollop out and popped it into his mouth. Tim found this incredibly rude, but Barnowl didn't flinch.

'Yes, yes, everything is fine, Greg,' replied Barnowl, smiling weakly at the England captain.

Tim was starting to find their relationship uncomfortable. Surely Barnowl, the England manager, should be in charge, but ever since they'd arrived, it felt like the other way round. Barnowl was clearly petrified of Punch.

Punch scooped the final dollop of Barnowl's chocolate mousse from the bowl and slowly licked it off his finger, making a horrible, loud smacking noise. Barnowl looked mournfully down at his empty bowl. It had been a really nice mousse.

'Lemme guess, you're asking the boss about those idiot llamas again,' said Punch.

'Might be,' replied Tim with a shrug. He was trying to be cool, but his forehead was starting to burn up like a marshmallow in a campsite fire.

'I'll be really upset if I have to say this again,' whispered Punch, leaning in closer to Tim so he could smell his chocolatey breath. 'Those llamas are going nowhere near this team, not if I have anything to do with it.'

Tim gulped. His back was getting really sweaty now. But he wasn't going to be threatened by this horrible footballer. 'That's up to the manager, not you,' he replied bravely.

Punch let out a huge roaring laugh, which made everyone in the hotel dining room turn and look at their table. 'Oh, yes of course,' he cackled sarcastically. 'That's exactly right, it's up to the manager.' He slapped Barnowl on the back. 'Isn't it, boss?'

Barnowl hunched forward, staring directly into his bowl. 'Yes, that's right,' he mumbled meekly.

'Now go on your way, llama boy,' said Punch, menacingly brandishing a spoon. 'We don't want this to get ugly, now do we?' Punch could make even spoons look threatening.

Tim's heart was banging so loudly against his chest, he was sure the whole room could hear it. Whatever Punch was threatening didn't sound good. His earlier bravery had gurgled away down the plughole. It was time to go. He left the hotel dining room as quickly as possible.

As he shuffled off down the long hotel corridor, trying to control his beating heart, Tim felt a small tug on the corner of his shirt. He looked down to see a tiny girl, who was maybe five or six. She was dressed from head to foot in full England kit. She had the white shirt, blue shorts and white socks. Her face was painted with the England flag and in her hands she proudly held an England football, which had a number of squiggly signatures all over it.

'Can you sign my ball, Tim?' asked the girl with a wide-eyed look of admiration.

'Er, erm . . . sure,' said Tim, taking the ball and the little marker pen the girl was holding out to him.

'I've got most of the team already, but I really wanted yours, and Cairo's, and your funny man in the cap. You and the llamas are my favourites,' continued the girl.

Tim smiled as he added his squiggly signature to one of the panels on the ball.

A large man in a matching England jersey appeared alongside the girl. He too was smiling broadly at Tim. 'We are both going to the match tomorrow,' said the man. 'I'm really hoping we can beat Panama. We *have* to beat them.'

'You can make us win,' said the girl as Tim handed the ball and the pen back to her.

'Erm, I'll try,' said Tim with a wince. After the conversation with Punch, it seemed unlikely.

'Good luck, we'll be rooting for ya,' said the man, and he warmly shook Tim's hand. Then his little girl stuck her hand out for a handshake. Tim shook it gently, sniffing back a little tear. This little girl and her dad were what it meant to be an England fan. Tim remembered he'd been exactly like this until he'd got so involved with it all. Everyone wanted to experience that feeling of sheer happiness when the team you support wins. That's what football is all about.

This was it for Tim. He *had* to find a way to make Barnowl and Punch listen. He wasn't going to stop until Barnowl started to play his llamas.

19
ENGLAND V PANAMA

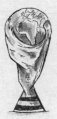

'*Y seremos así prez y gala . . . De este mundo feraz de Colón*,' sang the entire Panama team proudly as the sun bounced off their sparkling red shirts.

As expected, the England starting eleven contained no llamas. Jo Hussain-Bolt had replaced the injured Jack Chilly. Once again the llamas remained in the transporter with Cairo for company. You could cut the grumpiness in the transporter with a knife and spread it on toast. He was now telling his problems to Ludo, too.

'Oh, Ludo, why does Tim think football is the most important thing in the world?' Cairo mumbled sadly in Ludo's ear. 'That's all he thinks about and it's making him so angry. I wish the World Cup could end so I can get my real friend back. I really need to talk to him about something.'

Ludo stared at back at Cairo blankly.

It was still only Frank who seemed to be enjoying his World Cup experience. He sat high up in the stands with the rest of the England fans, singing, chanting, clapping and occasionally joining a conga line that snaked around the seats. However, he was concerned about the empty seat next to him, where McCloud should have been. The Scottish coach had vanished since the trouble in the hotel lobby with Barnowl. Where had he gone?

The Panama team looked really fired up as they began taking their positions ahead of kick-off. Beating their chests, hugging each other, jumping up and down heading imaginary footballs. The majority of the England team ambled about making the odd joke here and there to each other. Only T. J. Wilkinson looked focused, but nobody talked to him.

Tim had decided he wasn't going to sit at the back of the dugout behind all the subs; he was going to stand in the technical area on the side of the pitch. Barnowl wasn't happy with this, and hissed at him to sit down, but Tim ignored him. Nobody was going to manhandle a twelve-year-old back to his seat in front of a crowd of 50,000 and many millions watching on TV.

'C'mon, Jo, you can do this! Get one in early, make them know you're there!' shouted Tim to Jo Hussain-Bolt, who looked like he was just about to be run over by a tank. You could see his legs wobbling with fear at his first appearance in a World Cup match.

'Shut up, boy,' bellowed Greg Punch from the centre circle. 'I'll look after him. Keep it buttoned.'

Punch was true to his word. Hussain-Bolt's first touch of the ball saw him lifted a few feet up in the air as a Panama midfielder smashed into his legs. A hideous, bone-crunching foul.

'Play on,' shouted the ref.

Punch didn't need any further encouragement, he elbowed the Panama midfielder in the stomach. The midfielder crumpled to the ground in a heap.

'Play on,' shouted the ref.

The crowd gasped in astonishment. This wasn't a football match, it was a wrestling bout. This ref was clearly useless, and also scared of Greg Punch.

The game continued like this for ages. Panama were a hard team and seemed to revel in thundering challenges. The ref was happy to let the play flow even if it meant someone ending up in hospital.

It was still 0 – 0 at half-time. England's best chance came from a crafty run by Jim Hoisin, who dodged

three players before drilling a defence-splitting pass to Hussain-Bolt. But sadly the Nork Town striker was having a terrible first half and he tripped over trying to collect the ball, and the keeper quickly gobbled it up. Every manager in the world would have taken him off by now, but not Barnowl.

The second half was very similar to the first. Hussain-Bolt was totally off the pace. An oak tree standing on the edge of the area would have had more impact.

'You've got to take him off,' Tim pleaded with Barnowl in the sixtieth minute. 'He's done nothing all game. We have to win the match. We're never going to score with him on the pitch.'

For the slightest moment it appeared that Barnowl nodded at Tim, but then he looked at the pitch and his face went white as a sheet.

'Er . . . erm, I think he still has time to come good,' replied Barnowl.

'Unbelievable!' shouted Tim into the air and shaking his head 'What's wrong with you all?'

The England fans had started a loud chorus of boos. They were also demanding a substitute.

Despite all the carnage around him, Jim Hoisin was having a good game, dancing through sliding tackles as though they weren't there. It was a shame Hussain-Bolt wasn't on his wavelength. He just couldn't get to any of the killer balls Hoisin provided. Then, with just ten minutes to go, and with the crowd now screaming for a substitution, Barnowl's hand was forced.

A Panama defender elbowed Hussain-Bolt square in the face, challenging for a high ball, and knocked him out cold. The physios ran on to the pitch and tried to revive him, but to no avail. They did that spinning-arms move to the England bench, indicating for a substitute player.

This was Tim's moment. 'You've got to bring on Goal Machine! We've only got ten minutes left to win the game,' he pleaded with Barnowl.

Barnowl had turned his back on Tim and was looking at the rest of his subs.

'Start warming up, Steakhouse,' he said, pointing to the thirty-three-year-old utility player.

'You can't play Steakhouse, he's not a striker,' begged Tim.

'He's right, I'm not,' added Steakhouse cheerfully, removing his tracksuit. 'In fact I can't remember the last time I scored a goal . . . or had a shot on target.'

'Well, this is your big moment then, isn't it?' said

119

Barnowl through gritted teeth.

'The only way we are going to win this is with Goal Machine on the pitch,' pleaded Tim. He was nearly on his knees begging the England manager.

'He's got a point, boss,' added Steakhouse, giving Tim a wink.

'Listen to me, Steak—' Barnowl's next words were cut off by a huge roar from the crowd.

'GOAL MACHINE, GOAL MACHINE, GOAL MACHINE, GOAL MACHINE, GOAL MACHINE,' they bellowed with gathering ferocity.

'You've got to listen to the crowd,' pleaded Tim. 'This is your career at stake here.'

'GOAL MACHINE, GOAL MACHINE, GOAL MACHINE, GOAL MACHINE,' chanted the crowd. Even the dignitaries in the posh seats were shouting it.

Barnowl put his head in his hands. 'Do it,' he muttered.

Tim punched the air and sprinted off to collect Goal Machine. He was on the pitch in under a minute. Greg Punch stood in the middle of the pitch, his face looking like he'd just eaten a whole bag of lemons.

The crowd was at fever pitch now as the clock ticked down to the final whistle. Panama knew a point might be enough to squeak through to the second round on goal difference, but England needed to win. Panama moved everyone into their own half of the pitch. 'Defend at all costs,' was the instruction from their manager.

England huffed and puffed but they couldn't break through the wall of ten red shirts. Jim Hoisin tried everything in his skills-and-tricks locker, but everywhere he turned he found a Panama player blocking his way.

Even though Goal Machine was out of form, he looked lively and was creating havoc just running around the Panama players. Even without the ball he was being man-marked by three huge Panama defenders. I mean llama-marked. This gave the other England players a bit more space to play.

Then, as the fourth official raised the big orange digital display to show the additional one minute, T. J. Wilkinson found himself clear, with the ball at his feet. A mass of England shirts swarmed into the area. T. J. Wilkinson, under pressure from a Panama defender, sent a huge looping cross into the area. It was like someone had thrown a grenade into the box. White and red shirts scattered to and fro, tussling and battling to get to the ball. A hairy foot reached it first. Goal Machine flicking the ball towards the top right-hand corner of the goal. The keeper didn't see it in time.

'PINGGGGGGGGGGGGGGGG,' hollered the post as the ball cracked against its metal frame. Goal Machine had . . . MISSED!! Well, he wasn't in his usual goal-scoring mood, was he?

OH NO! The crowd let out another huge gasp, and then almost instantly a huge roar. The Panama net bulged as the ball was smashed into it. It was Greg Punch and his bullet-like forehead, who was following up Goal Machine's rebounding shot.

ENGLAND 1 – 0 PANAMA

The England players leaped on Punch as he held aloft his arms to receive the praise of the England crowd. Goal Machine didn't join in, and with a typical lack of interest, he swung his neck low to take a bite out of the juicy grass beneath him. Nobody came to congratulate him on his assist.

The ref put his whistle to his lips and blew for full-time. The England bench went wild and streamed on to the pitch to congratulate the rest of the team.

Tim bit the inside of his cheek. England had done it. They'd somehow qualified for the knockout phase. But Tim wasn't that pleased. It was Goal Machine

who'd made the difference, not that idiot Greg
Punch. He went up to Goal Machine, gave him a
stroke and whispered 'Well done' to him. The crowd
and England team were in the far corner of the pitch
going wild with celebration. Tim couldn't share their
joy. Things just didn't feel right.

20
THE VISITORS

Tim lay on his bed and stared blankly at the ceiling. The England team had returned from the Panama match about an hour ago and were already celebrating downstairs. Tim certainly didn't feel like joining them. Cairo was tending to the llamas and still not really talking to him, he hadn't seen McCloud since the hotel argument with Barnowl, and even his dad had disappeared somewhere. He had never felt this flat after winning a match before. He knew he'd have felt better if Goal Machine had scored, rather than the odious Greg Punch, and if Cairo and McCloud had been with him on the touchline celebrating like the good old days of their cup run last season.

The digital display on the hotel clock by his bed showed 7.14 p.m. He knew this was far too early for a twelve-year-old to go to sleep, but he had nothing better to do. The sun went down very quickly in

Mucho Plata, so at least it felt like proper night-time. He pulled the thin sheet over his body and clenched his eyes shut, waiting for sleep to arrive. He could feel his body starting to drift away.

Did the window just slide open? Was that a rustling in the corner? Was he already dreaming?

That was definitely another rustle from the corner, he thought . . . There it was again. Was someone trying to check whether he'd eaten that packet of biscuits you always get in a hotel room?

He quickly sat up and snapped on the bedside light, peering across the room to where the tea-making stuff was. There was nothing there, except a small plastic piece of packaging gently floating its way to the floor. Someone *had* been checking his biscuits! Lucky he had eaten them already.

Something tapped him on the shoulder.

'WHHHAAAΛAAAAAAAAA,' screamed Tim, jumping out of his skin. Whatever it was gave him the fright of his life. He spun round, and through the gloom he could make out a small figure dressed totally in black. A pair of piercing blue eyes blinked at him from a small slit in the black mask that covered its face.

'Made you look, made you stare, made you lose

your underwear,' chanted the figure with glee.

'Fi . . . Fi . . . o . . . na?' asked Tim, still trembling slightly.

'Yeah, it's me, Queen of the Ninjas,' she said, proudly whipping off her mask.

'What are you doing here?' spluttered Tim. 'I thought you were just the princess of the ninjas?'

'I've been promoted,' replied Fiona. 'I promoted myself. I've been brilliant recently, especially after solving the case of the missing milk.'

'I didn't know ninjas solved crimes.'

'I'm also a private investialligator,' replied Fiona.

'You mean "investigator".'

'I'm also one of them, too,' added Fiona, beating her chest.

There was a friendly tappity-tap at the hotel-room door. Tim jumped up and opened the door.

'SURPRISE!!!!' called the three figures standing in the corridor.

'Mum? . . . Monica? . . . Molly?' said Tim with surprise. Molly is Cairo's mum, in case you've forgotten.

The trio bustled past him and started settling themselves into the room, like families tend to do.

'Why are you all here?' said Tim. 'Dad said Molly was just bringing the llamas.'

'A hello would have been a nicer welcome,' said Beetroot as she began preparing cups of tea for everyone. This is always the first thing you should do when you get in from a long flight.

'Sorry . . . HELLO, everyone,' said Tim, trying to power as much energy into the welcome as he could, which wasn't much.

'The llamas are already settling in with Cairo outside,' said Molly, giving Tim a huge smile and a big hug. Tim had been in such a bad mood with Cairo, he had almost forgotten that his mum was one of the nice, cool mums you sometimes get. 'Cairo seems a bit down, though. Any idea what's up with him?'

Tim shrugged. He didn't want to tell Cairo's mum her son didn't seem to care about the most important football tournament in the world.

'We heard things weren't going too well for you and the llamas,' said Beetroot, wrestling the foil off one those tiny milk pots. Most of it squirted on the floor.

'How did you hear that? Did Dad tell you?' asked Tim.

Monica let out a large tut and rolled her eyes. 'How many times?' she said. 'Don't you ever use the Internet, watch the news, or check what's going on in the world?'

'Sort of,' said Tim with a shrug. 'It's a bit like living in a bubble here. They try and keep us away from the outside world. I know the fans aren't happy about the llamas not being in the team – I can hear the chanting, but really the only regular news we get is about chocolate mousse. It's a big deal here.'

'It certainly is a big deal,' said Fiona, through a mouthful of the thick chocolatey pudding she had found somewhere. 'Delicktious.'

Monica fetched her trusty laptop from out of her rucksack and began tapping away on it.

'There's loads of news about them, and it's all bad,' continued Monica. 'Not one positive story, even after they beat Panama. Everyone hates Ray Barnowl, even more than ever before, because he still won't pick the llamas.'

She spun her laptop round and presented Tim with a screenful of screaming headlines.

BARNOWL OUT!!!!
PUNCH SAVES BARNOWL'S SKIN!
BARNOWL THE TWIT TWIT TWOO!
SHOW BARNOWL THE BARNDOOR!
BARN OWL CATCHES LARGE MOUSE!

'Ignore that last one,' added Monica. 'Not sure how that slipped in there. Bit of an issue with the coding script.'

'But Barnowl's still in charge of the team,' said Tim, flopping back on to the bed. 'Apart from being forced to put Goal Machine on in the last few minutes of the Panama match, he doesn't want to play the llamas. I know he won't play them against Japan in the next round. He won't drop Punch and Badger for Cruncher and Ludo. He's scared of them, for some reason.'

'Surely that's not as important as two of the world's best football-playing llamas,' said Molly.

'Doesn't matter,' said Tim. 'Barnowl still picks the team. He won't pick them. It's like he's been hypnotized by Greg Punch.'

'Then we are going to have to make him pick them,' said Beetroot.

'How?' said Tim, punching a pillow. 'All the England fans and media are shouting for the llamas to be in the team, and Barnowl is *still* ignoring them. How are you lot going to change that?'

Nobody said anything for a few minutes. They just made a lot of pretending-to-think noises.

The window slid open and the small dark figure of Fiona, wrapped up in her ninja gear, began climbing out of it.

'And where do you think you are going, young lady?' asked Beetroot.

'The Empress of the Ninjas doesn't need to explain herself to mere mortals like you.'

'I thought you were just the Queen of the Ninjas?' said Tim.

'I've recently been promoted again,' replied Fiona smugly. 'After all, I am brilliant at my job.'

'May I ask where you are going again?' said Beetroot firmly, moving to shut the window.

'I've solved your problem,' she said with a cheeky smile, although you couldn't see it as it was behind her dark mask. 'I will be back to save the day very soon.'

Fiona hopped free of the window, expertly sliding it shut behind her, and vanished into the night.

'Aren't we on the fourth floor?' asked Tim. 'Won't she fall to her death?'

Beetroot, Monica and Molly looked at each other and shrugged.

'We've promised we can't reveal her ninja secrets,' said Monica with a heavy sigh.

'Or she'll sprinkle magic ninja dust in our baked potatoes,' added Beetroot.

'Magic . . . ninja dust?' asked Tim in disbelief.

'Lemon sherbet,' whispered Monica out of the corner of her mouth. 'Tastes horrible on potatoes. Not worth the argument.'

'Isn't Dad supposed to be here too?' asked Tim.

'Oh yes, he's here, he just waiting for Fi—' Beetroot clamped her hand over her mouth, stopping herself possibly revealing Fiona's secret method. 'Anyway, let's have some tea, shall we?'

Everyone nodded in agreement. Turning down the offer of a cup of tea is one of the most terrible things you can do.

21
TRAINING WITH THE LLAMAS

The next day, the number of TV camera crews and newspaper journalists camped outside the hotel had trebled in size. There was also a strong contingent of England fans who had built a small campsite city to live in. Despite England's last-minute winner against Panama, they were all really angry. The greengrocer from outside the England HQ had left his spot with the England cricket team and had travelled to Mucho Plata. He was fully stocked with all kinds of amazing fruit ready to be hurled.

The pressure felt like a huge iron overcoat on Barnowl's shoulders. He knew he couldn't keep the llamas in exile during today's training session, with all the media and England fans watching close-by. There would be a riot if he left them to train on their own again.

So he agreed to allow Tim to bring the llamas to

the first squad training, a few days before the crucial (everything is crucial during the World Cup) second-round match with Japan, who had somehow finished top of their tough group.

Tim proudly escorted the four llamas, and Motorway, on to the England training pitch. He could feel at least nineteen sets of England-player eyeballs staring intently at them. Then, just as everyone was getting used to seeing four llamas and a sheep on the training pitch, Cairo and Molly emerged with another seven llamas – Bill, Brian, Barcelona, Bob, Smasher, Dasher and the Duke. All the team were back together, and they were loving it. Even Cairo was grinning from ear to ear. Having his mum and the llamas arrive had given him something to be happy about for the first time in ages.

Bob had the biggest, most elaborate holiday haircut you could ever imagine: shaved down one side, with a huge spike at the top and corn rows on the other. The Duke had what looked like a gold bow tie around his neck. Dasher had the word 'PARTY' shaved into her coat. Bill and Brian were wearing sunglasses, and Barcelona was moon-walking again. Smasher brought up the rear. There was nothing unusual about him. He didn't like a fuss.

'We thought we'd fancy them up a bit, hope you don't mind,' Molly called to Tim. 'After all, they are on holiday and they are not in the team, so they can do what they like.'

Tim's four England team llamas were clearly delighted to see their friends again and ran among them joyfully. Even Ludo, who rarely got excited, because he was a calm and solid keeper, was thrilled in his own llama way, nodding his appreciation to the rest of his teammates.

The great atmosphere didn't last long.

'You're not welcome here, llamas!' Greg Punch shouted across the pitch. 'We can win this World Cup without your help.'

The llamas ignored the jibes from Punch, because they are llamas. But Tim felt it like an arrow in the back. Cairo's good mood was also quickly washed away.

'Take them away, llama boys, nobody wants them,' continued Punch.

A gaggle of players around him started hooting and making moo-ing noises. Tim clenched his fists, digging his thumbs into the palms of his hands until it hurt. He had to control his rising anger.

'Hey, leave them alone, you bullies!' shouted Molly.

'And what's that sheep doing here?' goaded Punch, ignoring Molly's protests. 'Sheep are the stupidest animals around, after llamas . . . and little boys.'

That was it. Tim snapped. He left the llamas and sprinted the length of the pitch towards the England players. Cairo quickly followed, but he wasn't as fast as his friend. Molly was left to prevent the llamas stampeding after them.

'Oooo! Here comes a little boy, ready to knock me out,' Punch laughed as Tim charged towards him.

Tim was running at full tilt, fuelled by the anger pulsing through his body. But he was out of breath by the time he reached the horrible England captain.

Then he realized he wasn't actually sure what he was going to do.

'You . . . you . . . take that back,' puffed Tim when he finally reached Punch, putting his hands on his knees to help gather some air into his lungs.

Cairo lumbered over a few seconds later. He felt like he'd just run a marathon. He couldn't speak at all. All those chocolate mousses had made him really unfit.

Punch laughed and pretended to quiver in fear. 'I never take anything back,' he said menacingly. 'I'm the England captain. You should be respecting me.'

Tim had regained his composure, but he still wasn't that sure what he should do next. His index finger suddenly shot out and prodded Punch in the chest, he hadn't meant to do that. Had his index finger gone mad? What was it doing?

'It's time you learned to train with our llamas,' said Tim as bravely as he could, his finger still prodding Punch's chest. He couldn't make it stop.

Punch looked down slowly at Tim's finger. His face twisted with rage, and his teeth appeared like sharp yellow soldiers stepping out from behind two pink curtains. 'Why . . . are . . . you . . . touching . . . me?' he said in a low and menacing tone.

'Erm . . .' Tim slowly withdrew his finger, took a step back and repeated his bold statement, but this time in a squeak. 'Train with my llamas?'

'Nobody tells Greg Punch what to do,' said Punch, and he raised his hands as if to give to Tim a massive shove in chest.

Tim stumbled backwards a few steps, and then his legs gave way and he tumbled to the ground, completely startled. Some of the players joined Punch in howls of laughter.

Punch started advancing towards him. Tim closed his eyes. What was he going to do next? Kick him over the crossbar?

Tim heard a scuffle break out above him, and looked up. Standing between Punch and Tim was T. J. Wilkinson, Cairo – and now Ludo, who had escaped Molly's restraints. The three of them were pushing and jostling to get Punch away from Tim.

'What are you doing? You can't shove a twelve-year-old boy!' exclaimed T. J. Wilkinson.

'Why not? This is a man's game. You going to stop me, bookworm? Anyway, I didn't, he fell over,' replied Punch, struggling to break free.

'You are mad in the head,' shouted Cairo, trying to barge Punch away with his shoulder. He wasn't getting very far. It felt like he was up against a brick wall.

'Shut up, boy,' shouted Punch at Cairo.

That was clearly it for Ludo. He gave a massive snort and butted Greg Punch right in the chest. Punch staggered back and began to cough and splutter. Ludo readied himself for a return attack, but Punch thought better of it. A nasty snarl was all he could come up with.

'You need to give these guys a break,' said T. J. Wilkinson, helping Tim to feet. 'That Goal Machine llama helped save our bacon against Panama.'

'Pfftttt,' replied Punch. '*I* saved our bacon. *I* scored the winning goal.' Punch took a long look at Ludo, who was still eyeballing him, then shook his head and stalked off, muttering under his breath, the majority of the England players following him.

'You OK, kid?' said T. J. Wilkinson to Tim. 'Sorry about him, he's always been a bully. I would say he gets better when you get to know him, but he doesn't.'

'Thanks,' said Tim. 'To be honest, I didn't know what I was doing. I just want help England win the World Cup, and I think our llamas can do that.'

'You clearly weren't thinking,' said Cairo with a

scowl. 'Getting Ludo into a fight . . . he could have been really injured!'

'I didn't get him into the fight,' replied Tim, his cheeks flushing red. 'He came to help out.'

'You started the fight by prodding that Punch bloke,' said Cairo. 'All this football stress is giving you a massive temper.'

'IT IS NOT!!!' barked Tim.

T. J. Wilkinson coughed, and tried to change the subject, looking at Ludo. 'He certainly is an impressive animal. I don't think I've been this close to a llama before. Can I touch him?'

'Yes, I think he'll let you. He knows you are a good person,' said Cairo.

'Wow, that's really soft wool, it's like a duvet,' he said, patting the side of Ludo's neck tentatively. 'I think I'd like to train with the llamas. I can probably get some of the rest of the team to join as well – at least the ones who aren't in Punch's gang.'

'Like who?' asked Tim.

'Probably most of the squad players. They're getting a bit fed up sitting on the bench all the time. Punch has his favourites and always picks them, however badly they play.'

'You mean, *Barnowl* has his favourites,' said

Tim, correcting T. J. Wilkinson.

A wry smile crossed T. J. Wilkinson's face, and he shook his head.

'If you think that Barnowl picks this team, then you've got a lot to learn.'

'I *knew* there was something funny going on with Punch and Barnowl,' said Tim.

'Leave it with me, chief . . . and I'll see you later, big guy.' He gave Ludo one last tickle under the chin and jogged off to find the rest of the squad.

22
LLAMA UNITED AGAIN

T. J. Wilkinson had been true to his word, and had gathered six more England players to train with the llamas the next day. Greg Punch took the other players, the ones in the first team, with him to train on the other side of the hotel. Ray Barnowl was nowhere to be seen. Someone said he was spending time with the toilet. All that chocolate mousse can take its toll.

Tim ran some 'partner drills' to try and get the llamas and human players to gel. They were suspicious of each other at first, but eventually Tim's tactic paid off and at the end of the session they had the most amazing training match.

The 'holiday llamas', as I'm going to call the ones who weren't in the World Cup squad, watched from the sidelines. They got bored very quickly and began trying to discover ways into the crop of buildings that backed on to the training pitches. The grounds team's tea hut had its door kicked in, and the shed with all the tractors had its flat roof peeled off. The only place they couldn't get into was the hotel's chocolate mousse storage barn. There was an open window at the very top, but it was too high for the llamas, so they had to make do with having a tug-of-war with a blue-and-white piece of cloth that looked suspiciously like a pair of pants.

Under a tree, on the edge of the training pitch, Cairo and his mum, Molly, took a break from looking after the llamas and shared a cooling raspberry milkshake.

'You feeling OK, Cairo?' asked Molly. 'You seem a bit down.'

'It's nothing,' replied Cairo with a sigh. 'Everything is fine.'

'Cairo Helsinki Anderson . . .' said Molly.

Cairo knew he was in trouble when she used his full name. Yes, his surname is Anderson. Oh, the 'Helsinki' bit? Molly loves to travel: Cairo and Helsinki are two of her favourite capitals.

'. . . You know you can't keep anything from me. We've been on our own for twelve years; you can't be keeping secrets from me.'

Cairo puffed out his cheeks and then drained the rest of the milkshake. He then launched into a long rant about how Tim didn't understand that there was more to life than football, that Tim had been mean to him on the football pitch, told him he was rubbish at looking after animals, got Ludo into a fight and was now getting angry at everything. He also disrespected his baby hedgehog.

Molly sat and listened to every word her son said, then gave him a kiss on the forehead and a big hug.

'Sometimes friends fall out over lots of things,' she said calmly. 'But your friendship will come through this. Tim is under a lot of pressure with the World Cup and is concentrating on that. Football can cloud people's judgement – I know all about that. The tournament is only on for a few weeks, I'm sure he'll return to normal after that.' She patted Cairo gently on the leg. 'And remember, you've been incredibly important in looking after the llamas and getting them to the World Cup. I'm sure Tim will soon realize how valuable you are to the team.'

Cairo nodded uncertainly and looked out over the training pitch, where Tim was jabbering away excitedly to T. J. Wilkinson.

'The good thing is, all the llamas are back together, happy and in top form,' continued Molly. 'I don't think we should ever split them up again. The seven that were left behind were in a mood all week . . .'

Cairo stared into the bottom of his empty glass. He had one other thing on his mind that had been troubling him, and it was nothing to do with Tim. Cairo had never met his dad and knew nothing about him, apart from seeing half a photo of him – unfortunately, only the bottom half: a pair of legs. Legs he thought he'd recently seen. He took a deep breath, knowing it was an uncomfortable subject for his mum.

'I've been thinking about that half-picture of Dad we have at home somewhere,' said Cairo. 'I've been thinking about it since I bumped into someone the other day who had really similar legs. And it reminded me of the photo.'

'Oh, really?' said Molly, not sounding her usual confident self. 'It's hard to tell someone from just their legs.'

'I can't get it out of my head,' said Cairo. 'Especially as I haven't really had anyone to talk to, to take my mind off it.'

Molly sighed. 'I think it's time we went inside,' she said, gathering up her things and the empty raspberry milkshake glass.

'MUM!' said Cairo firmly. 'Why do you always dodge questions about Dad?'

'He left us before you were born,' replied Molly, her voice also hardening. 'He just walked out. His job was going badly, so he claimed he had to leave to make it more successful.'

'What was his job?'

Molly paused again, sighed and sat back down. Letting Cairo go to the World Cup was always going to be risky, especially as he would be so close to the truth, without even knowing it.

'He was a footballer,' said Molly eventually. 'Actually, he still is a footballer, a very famous one.'

Cairo's eyes widened. Was his mum about to

confirm all those jumbled thoughts that had been rattling around in his brain since he met that rude German goalkeeper before the first match of the World Cup?

Molly rummaged around in her large handbag and, eventually, produced the half of the photo of Cairo's dad's legs that he had seen before. Cairo swiped it off her and began studying it.

Molly then delved deeper into her handbag and dug around in its darkest compartments, where thirty-year-old lipsticks and scrunched-up tissues lurked. She really needed to clean out her handbag. After what seemed like a hundred years, she revealed the other half of the torn photo and hesitantly handed it over to Cairo.

Cairo carefully matched the two halves together and gazed at the person in front of him.

The young man grinning back at them was Karl-Heinz Torstooper, the Golden Octopus, the best goalkeeper in the world with over two hundred caps for Germany and a trophy cabinet groaning with silverware. Although, when the picture was taken, he was just Karl-Heinz Torstooper: no legendary nickname, no Germany caps and no trophy cabinet.

Cairo leaped to his feet and took several lungfuls of air. 'My . . . DAD . . . is a world-famous goalkeeper?'

Molly nodded solemnly.

'Why didn't you tell me?'

'Because I was worried he would hurt you. He was too bothered with football to think about a family. Football was the most important thing.'

'He told you that?'

'Well, not exactly. I've not spoken to him since he walked out on us.'

'Does he even know about me?' asked Cairo. He began clambering to his feet. 'I've got to go and find him; it could be the biggest surprise and best news he's ever had,' he added excitedly, firing his words out like a machine gun. 'Great talk, Mum, love you loads. I've got to go.'

'Wait! You can't just go. What about the llamas?' Molly said urgently. 'We've got to help Tim with training and, Cairo . . . I don't want you to get your hopes up.'

'I know, I know. But I have to speak to my dad. I've never met the man, apart from that time in the tunnel when he wasn't very nice.' Cairo's words were gushing from his mouth like a waterfall.

'He *was* nice, but football took over,' said Molly sorrowfully.

'Please let me go, Mum . . . *please*,' begged Cairo. 'The llamas will be fine. They're happy now everyone is back together and you're here. Tim doesn't need me either.'

Molly bowed her head and rubbed her eyes. She wanted to say no, but she knew it would crush Cairo, especially as he'd had such a rough time of it lately. She let out a long sigh.

'OK, I suppose it's OK to go and find him,' she said. 'But you get one of the hotel staff to drive you to the Germany camp and you need to ring me as soon as you get there, then every half an hour you are there, then when you are on your way back here. Actually . . . just keep in touch all the time.'

'Yes, yes, OK. Thank you, Mum!' said Cairo.

He began sprinting away, waving to his mum as he left.

'This is not a good idea . . .' Molly called after him, but it was too late. He had already gone.

23
THE SECOND ROUND: ENGLAND V JAPAN

T. J. Wilkinson's claim that Barnowl didn't really pick the team seemed to ring true when the team was selected for the first knockout game of the World Cup against Japan. Barnowl had officially made one change, and it wasn't a positive one. T. J. Wilkinson had been dropped. It was a truly bonkers decision. T. J. Wilkinson was easily one of the best players in the team.

Tim sat in the changing room before the match and marvelled at how underprepared everyone seemed. All the players Tim thought *should* have been in the team were on the bench. Most of the selected team played for Greg Punch's Nork Town, the club that had bullied and cheated its way to the league title a few week earlier, with Greg as the captain.

'Why aren't you in the team?' said Tim quietly to T. J. Wilkinson.

'It's all the training with the llamas,' whispered T. J. Wilkinson, without looking up from the book he was reading. 'Punch thinks I've betrayed him.'

'What did Barnowl say about that?'

'Nothing, as usual. Once Punch tells him to do something, he does it.' He shrugged and turned back to his book.

It couldn't be clearer. This wasn't an England team, it was the Greg Punch XI. These players clearly weren't good enough to play international football, but Punch was such a bully he had intimidated the England manager to get him and his clubmates into the team. He'd done it for Nork Town, it would be easy to do it for England. The media pressure to force Barnowl to select some llamas in the team would have mucked up Punch's plans, and that's why he hated them so much.

Barnowl entered the changing room and made a feeble 'cough-cough' noise, trying to calm the noisy atmosphere.

'So, we are playing Japan today,' said Barnowl with all the power of a springbok trying to persuade some lions that they shouldn't eat him. 'We all know that Japan are rubbish at football, they've never won a major tournament and their main sport

151

is that thing in the nappies.'

'Babies,' added Steve Crispy unhelpfully.

'Sumo, you fool,' muttered Sid Melonhead. 'Sumo.'

'Who would have thought Japan would get this far?' continued Barnowl with a chuckle. 'Not me, that's for sure. I don't even know who takes their free kicks.'

Tim slapped his own forehead in amazement.

'Perhaps it's because Japan are actually quite good at football now,' said Tim bravely. 'They have been for a while. It's a very popular sport there, and has been for a few decades.' He was fed up with Barnowl's rubbish team talks. He looked around for support, but nobody backed him up. With Cairo looking for his dad, McCloud missing, presumed swimming in chocolate mousse somewhere, and the rest of the family already in their seats, Tim had no support whatsoever. He once again felt totally alone.

Barnowl paused and looked at Tim, trying to think of a comeback. But he didn't have time. There was a huge commotion at one of the windows at the top of the changing room. The window shook several times and then a glass pane was dislodged and smashed on to the floor.

Bob's amazing haircut and big hairy face poked through the window and let out a staggeringly loud burp.

'. . . UUUUURRRRRRRPPPPPPPPPPPPP . . .'

It went on for so long, T. J. Wilkinson had time to finish the chapter in his book.

'GET THAT LLAMA OUT OF HERE,' bellowed Punch, leaping to his feet.

Molly's face appeared, and she wrestled Bob away from the window.

'Sorry, sorry, sorry,' she said. 'It's really hard keeping eleven llamas in the transporter. They really want to be on the pitch.'

'GET THAT LLAMA OUT OF HERE,' Punch shouted again.

Molly gave Punch a really surprised, yet disdainful look. 'Cor, you're a moody one, aren't you?'

She didn't wait to hear Punch's response, and dragged Bob back to the trailer.

Punch kicked over a table of drinks and growled loudly.

The awkward silence was broken by a bell ringing, summoning the team to go out on to the pitch and start the match. The England players stood up and gingerly left the room. Tim had time to ask T. J.

Wilkinson one more question before he joined the subs' bench.

'Why does Greg Punch hate llamas so much?'

T. J. Wilkinson shrugged. 'Dunno, really,' he said. 'He's one of those people who doesn't get on with any animals. Once, on tour in South Africa, a baboon broke into his hotel room and threw a massive poo at him. He wasn't best pleased with that.'

Tim chuckled. That baboon deserved a medal.

24
SCOTTISH SAVIOUR

Forty-seven minutes later, the England team were back in the changing room. Half-time score:

ENGLAND 0 – 2 JAPAN

The players looked like they had been run over by a steamroller.

Tim sat quietly on one of the benches. He was so angry, he could hardly breathe. This was England's last chance and they were blowing it. He felt totally helpless.

The crowd outside were going wild and not in a good way. They had started hurling abuse at Barnowl from the first minute of the game and weren't stopping during the break. There was a heavy drumming sound from the seats above the changing rooms, as though the fans were trying to bash down the walls with medieval battering rams.

Barnowl looked very stressed when he re-entered

the changing room. His hair and suit were soaking wet. Someone had thrown a whole pint of milk over him as he entered the tunnel. I know. Who brings milk to a football match?

'So, we've had better first halves of football,' began Barnowl, wringing milk out of his tie.

As Tim rolled his eyes, waiting for another uninspiring team talk, he heard a window slide open.

'I think we should try and have a shot on the Japan goal this half, really test their keeper,' continued Barnowl, failing miserably to encourage his team.

'BARNOWL,' came a familiar voice from the corner of the room. 'STOP RIGHT THERE.'

Barnowl gulped. The voice sent a shiver down his spine.

'YOUR TIME IS OVER, BARNOWL,' said the black-clad figure of Fiona as she strolled confidently into the middle of the changing room.

'What do you want?' he asked, his voice trembling. He was expecting her to tell everyone about his lucky unicorn pants.

'I have here a letter from the governing body. They, and everyone in the world, want you out. You are a rubbish manager.'

Greg Punch stood up and snatched the letter from Fiona's outstretched hand. He read it very slowly to the group. He wasn't a great reader, so it took him ages. Here's what it said:

Hi there, Ray,
Sorry about this, but we are not really sure you should be the England manager any more. The team aren't very good, and you won't pick the llamas, and we were sort of hoping you would do that, because they are really good and the fans love them.

We have also been told that your team selections haven't actually been your own, and that's probably not great managing, is it?

So sorry, I hope you won't hold it against us and we can still be friends.

If you could leave the car keys and those
two really nice suits in your hotel room
before you check out, that would be great.

Cheerio,
The Governing Body

PS. We gave the letter to the little girl to
deliver because we didn't want to see you all
sad. Also, she wouldn't stop knocking on our
hotel-room doors and it kept us up at night.
Not getting enough sleep makes us really
grumpy in the morning. Hope you don't mind.

'That means you are sacked,' said Fiona. 'Collect
your things, and go to jail.'

Greg Punch started laughing. 'It doesn't say *when*
he should go, and besides, anyone could have written
this and put it on some headed notepaper. I think
Ray's got another half to manage. Security, remove
this silly little girl.'

Five no-neck security guards closed in on Fiona
and lifted her up by the shoulders. She began
thrashing her legs and arms about, and managed to
land a few lusty blows to the security guards' rock-
hard stomachs.

'Let her go,' came a familiar Scottish voice from
the changing-room doorway.

'YOU . . . AGAIN?' barked Barnowl. 'I TOLD YOU TO STAY AWAY FROM ME.'

Tim noticed McCloud look a bit sheepish. He held his hand out towards Barnowl. Barnowl looked at it suspiciously.

'I've been livin' in a chocolate mousse barn over the last few days, so I've had time tae think, and I'm here tae apologize,' said McCloud, keeping his firm hand stuck out, waiting for it to be shaken. 'I was wrong all those years ago. It was a rubbish tackle and I'm ashamed of it. It will haunt me furever.'

'A chocolate mousse barn?' was all Barnowl could say, his face still contorted with anger.

'Aye,' replied McCloud, looking slightly ashamed. 'I couldnae face the team, I was too embarrassed, but I couldnae leave them, so I hid in the chocolate mousse barn by the training pitch. The llamas worked out I was in there sharpish. They kept walkin' round it.'

McCloud turned to look at Tim. 'I'm sorry I left you in the lurch too, laddie,' he said.

Tim wasn't used to hearing such emotion from McCloud. Most of his stories were about him scoring the winner in a crucial match or making a vital goal-line clearance. Tim was seeing a different McCloud for the first time. He must have eaten too much chocolate mousse.

'The pitch was a mud bath,' McCloud went on. 'So slippy, like an ice rink. I wasnae a rough player, I just went in a bit quick on ma sliding tackle and instead of gettin' the fitba', I whacked into yer knee. Ah'm sorry for the whole affair. I've been a dunderheed. Will ye forgive me?'

Barnowl's face began to soften towards McCloud, and it looked like he was going to cry. 'I will accept your apology,' he said with a sniff, taking McCloud's hand and shaking it.

One positive thing can be said about footballers: they are very honourable when it comes to apologies.

 Three slow, sarcastic handclaps came from the other side of the changing room. It was Greg Punch. Who else.

'Well, boo-hoo, two old men make friends again,' said Punch in a mocking tone.

'We're about to start the second half. Barnowl, give us the team talk.'

McCloud looked embarrassed again. 'Ach, well, I have some news on that too,' he said. 'Wee Fiona is correct, and the letter she brought is official. I spoke to the governing body aboot Barnowl not being properly in charge of the team.'

'And how did you come to that theory?' asked Punch with a sneer.

'In the chocolate mousse barn. Ye can hear a lot when you are high up in a chocolate mousse barn. Late at night I could hear Barnowl being threatened not to pick the llamas in the team. I guess those threats came from you an' yer cronies.'

Punch and a handful of the players looked down at their feet. They didn't reply.

'See, I told you it was real,' said Fiona, sticking her tongue out at Punch.

'I have good an' bad news for you, Ray,' said McCloud, breathing in sharply before continuing: 'The governing body has made Tim and me joint England head coaches for the rest of the World Cup.'

Tim wasn't sure if this was the good or the bad news. Rather than looking crushed, like you'd expect when you'd been sacked, Barnowl looked relieved.

The stress of the job was clearly too much. Being threatened every day just isn't good for you.

'Oh,' was all he could say.

'But, the good news is they've given you a ten-million pound pay-off,' added McCloud, waving a large cheque in the air.

Football is one of the few jobs in the world where they give you a load of money when they sack you. Sadly, this doesn't happen if you are a bus driver or work in a sandwich shop.

A broad grin spread across Barnowl's face. He snatched up the cheque and planted a big kiss on it. The cheque did not enjoy this at all. No cheques do. What *is* a cheque? Good question.

'YIPPEEEE, YIPPEEEE, I'm free, I'm free!' shouted Barnowl, leaping about the room. 'I can leave this awful, stressful job, and open up a chocolate mousse shop.'

'I think you can probably open about a hundred with that much dosh,' remarked McCloud.

'Cheerio, losers,' he called to the rest of the room as he left ' . . . and *ththththththththththfffffppppt!!!* to you, Punch.' He blew a massive raspberry at the England captain. 'You can't blackmail me any more. I don't need you to get me the top football jobs, because

I'm never going to have to be a football manager ever again.'

Barnowl skipped and danced through the door, leaving the room in stunned silence.

After a long pause, Tim realized everyone was now looking directly at him. Ten minutes ago he had been sitting at the back of the dugout with nobody listening to him. Now he was the joint England head coach. They had forty-five minutes to win the game and save the country from humiliation. No pressure, then!

Tim's teeth clacked together in total panic. Inside his head it felt as though a load of monkeys were pulling all the wires out of his brain. That sick feeling he'd had when he was made goalkeeper in the Cup semi-final last season started to swamp his stomach.

The bell for the second half rang.

'Do it,' whispered Fiona from beside him. 'Be the England head coach. Make some substitutions.'

McCloud was nodding alongside her. He hadn't been involved in any llama or England player training as he'd been hiding in the chocolate mousse barn, so didn't have a good idea of the dynamics. It was all down to Tim.

Tim cleared his throat. The sick was beginning

to rise up. He couldn't be sick in front of all these people . . . He was the England head coach!

'Get a grip on yourself,' whispered Fiona, poking Tim firmly in a soft bit of his back. 'Or I'll break your games console.'

He took a deep breath. 'OK, I'm going to make some subs. We are going to a four-four-two formation. Goal Machine on for Hussain-Bolt, Cheeks off for Lightning and, er . . .' Tim paused and looked around the room. He had one more sub to make and two llamas available. Replace the keeper or replace a midfielder? He saw Punch snarling at him. That helped him make up his mind. '. . . and Cruncher for Punch.'

Punch's snarl dropped, and his face went totally blank, apart from a piercing stare that Tim could feel burning a hole in his forehead. It was a brave call by the twelve-year-old England head coach. But he had to do it. Cruncher was a much better player.

'Oh, and Steakhouse, you are the new captain,' added Tim as they trooped out of the changing room.

'Really!?' said Chaz Steakhouse. 'I'm not much of a captain.' Steakhouse gulped. He was about to have the game of his life.

25
ENGLAND V JAPAN:
(SECOND HALF)

The crowd erupted when Tim and McCloud arrived in the dugout without Barnowl. They made an even bigger noise when they realized Goal Machine, Lightning and Cruncher would be starting the half. They immediately starting chanting 'GOAL MACHINE . . . GOAL MACHINE . . . GOAL MACHINE.' The England fans weren't any better at thinking up songs than the Llama United fans.

The Japanese players were alarmed by the introduction of the three llamas. They clearly hadn't planned for this.

At first, the England players didn't really know what to do with them either. They continued to play as if the llamas weren't there. Luckily it was the new captain, Chaz Steakhouse, the only human player on the pitch who had trained with the llamas, who suddenly found himself responsible for the entire team.

Winning the ball in the Japanese midfield, he drilled the finest pass of his career to Lightning, who was galloping down the right wing. She controlled the ball expertly with her right foot, took one more touch to steady herself, and fired a beautiful cross into the area. The Japanese keeper clutched at thin air as the ball was volleyed in at the far post by the onrushing Goal Machine.

ENGLAND 1 – 2 JAPAN

They were back in the game! Tim turned to celebrate with Cairo, remembering with a shock that he wasn't there. He'd been so wrapped up in the match, he hadn't even noticed his best friend hadn't arrived for the game. He looked to McCloud, who casually nodded back at him, removed his right hand from his pocket and gave him a tiny thumbs-up. He was as cool as a cucumber.

England piled on the pressure, and in the eighty-first minute it finally paid off. Cruncher won the ball on the edge of the Japanese area and curled home a sublime equalizer. The keeper had no chance. What a strike –

ENGLAND 2 – 2 JAPAN!!

Cruncher gobbled up the entire corner flag as a celebration and was booked by the referee.

The England fans went mad, while the Japan fans and players were on their knees. What an amazing comeback!

Tim jumped up and punched the air, then quickly composed himself. He knew England could win this now. It was Lightning who made the difference. With the ball at her feet she drove deep into the heart of the Japanese defence, dancing her way into the area, tricking three players into going in the totally wrong direction. Then she did something very unusual: she unselfishly passed the ball into the path of onrushing defender Sid Melonhead, one of Greg Punch's gang of cronies. This was the first time a llama had passed to someone they didn't know. Melonhead couldn't believe his luck and gleefully slammed the ball into the back of the net from three yards.

ENGLAND 3 – 2 JAPAN!!!!

Melonhead had time to graciously nod his approval to Lightning before he was swamped by his delighted teammates. Lightning leaned down and took a big bite out of the penalty spot.

A warm glow of satisfaction spread all over Tim as he calmly took his seat in the dugout next to McCloud. Nerves? What nerves? He felt like a real international manager now. The final whistle blew seconds later. Tim looked up into the jubilant England fans in the stands. He could see his dad, mum and Monica waving frantically back at him. Fiona sat calmly alongside them, devouring her fifth chocolate mousse of the day. Molly led the 'holiday llamas' on to the pitch and let them mingle with the llama match winners, much to the annoyance of the groundsmen, who were fed up that their beautiful pitch was now having even more huge clumps of juicy turf munched out of it.

The only person still missing was Cairo. Tim looked at the empty seat next to him. He couldn't understand it. Why would Cairo not even turn up to such an important World Cup match?

'This is just the start, Tim,' said McCloud. 'Some bigger mountains to climb in the next few rounds.'

'Aye,' replied Tim. 'Er . . . I mean yes.'

'Yer look a bit peely-wally there, laddie,' said McCloud.

'Eh?'

'Have yer boaked?'

'Eh?'

'Bin sick?'

'Oh . . . no,' said Tim. 'I don't feel sick at all. I'm a top international manager now . . . cool and calm.'

McCloud smiled. 'Just Brazil, then maybe Argentina, and then probably Germany in the final to get through after that.'

Tim felt his stomach lurch forward and then backwards.

'OK, where's the toilet?' he groaned, cupping his hand over his mouth.

26
GERMAN HQ

Cairo was sitting at a large oak table in the middle of Karl-Heinz Torstooper's plush hotel suite. He was munching his way through a huge plate of food, including many things he'd never eaten before. Slabs of thick meat, potatoes, boiled dumplings and pickled vegetables.

'This German food will make you stronger,' said Heinrich Prussia, sitting next to him. 'Your legs are weak and feeble. This will give you the raw power you need to become like Torstooper, the greatest player ever to walk the face of the planet. You will become a strong German, not a puny Englishman, like the players on their terrible team.'

Unhelpfully, Prussia spoke to Cairo in German *and* English, which made it very confusing, but I'm just going to translate it straight into English or we'll be here all day. Anyway, half the time Cairo hadn't a clue what this strange man was talking about.

It was Torstooper's agent, Prussia, who had let Cairo explain his story about being Torstooper's son when he had arrived at the hotel looking for him. He was also the one who had convinced the Golden Octopus that it must be true. They had a long discussion in German on the balcony outside the plush suite, where Prussia waved his walking stick about a lot. After that, Prussia did most of the talking, while Torstooper eyed his newly discovered son as though he was a really complicated box of Lego.

The German manager, Geoff Coren, now entered the room, balancing on a giant pair of thick, high-heeled cowboy boots. They didn't make him that much taller. He still only reached Torstooper's armpit. Coren had just masterminded a 4 – 0 win over Colombia in their second-round match, but now he had other things on his mind.

'So England managed to get into the quarter-

171

finals somehow,' he said, throwing a World Cup wall chart on to the table with disgust. 'Looking at this, if everything goes to plan we will only have to face England again in the final in the Big Sparkly Diamond Stadium.'

'This is an impressive stadium for Torstooper to play in, when Torstooper's team reach the final,' said Torstooper confidently to Coren. He had to speak in English to Coren, as Coren couldn't speak German either.

Prussia made a cynical *ppfffittt* noise under his breath. He had no respect for Coren and didn't believe England were good enough to get anywhere near the World Cup final.

'I'm worried that with those llamas in the team, England *will* get to the final,' said Coren. 'We have to beat them. It is very important to me, after what happened with those llamas in the Cup.' He flicked a small tear away from the corner of his eye. That defeat had really hurt him, even though he'd tried to cheat.

'You got walloped by Llama United,' said Cairo, gulping back another mouthful of mash with sauerkraut on the top.

Coren hadn't really noticed the boy sitting by

Prussia before now. It suddenly dawned on him who it was. 'YOU!!' he exclaimed, storming over to the table and getting as close as possible to Cairo's face. Football managers seem to like getting really close and shouting 'YOU', don't they? I've no idea why. 'Why are *you* here? . . . You are part of the England coaching team!'

'The boy is Torstooper's son,' said Prussia, placing his hand coldly on Cairo's shoulder. 'He is very lucky to be the son of Torstooper, so will be spending time with the Germany team as the England team no longer wanted him.'

Cairo scrunched up his eyes quizzically at Prussia's statement. He couldn't remember actually agreeing to join the Germany team. He just wanted to meet his dad, and maybe have some nice food. Everything else was a bit odd, especially Prussia.

'Is this true?' asked Coren. 'You are his son?'

'Yes. He was my mum's boyfriend when he lived in England when he was younger,' said Cairo. 'I only found out the other day.'

'But you'll tell England all our secret plans and tactics,' said Coren. He seemed convinced that Cairo was a spy.

Cairo had started digging into a huge serving of

173

Apfelstrudel mit Sahne. That's a German apple pastry with cream.

'Hhmm, that's unlikely,' he said, casually licking up a blob of cream that had landed on his hand. 'Firstly, I don't really know anything about football or football tactics. Secondly, Tim and I aren't really talking at the moment.'

'What about the llamas? I thought you cared about the llamas?' asked Coren, eyeing Cairo suspiciously. 'I can't be losing to llamas again – it will ruin my career and my reputation.'

'I do still care about the llamas, but I'm not worried about them. My mum is here to look after them. She's an even bigger animal expert than me. I want to spend time getting to know my dad.'

He looked over at Torstooper, who tried to force a weak smile back at his son. Smiling wasn't really something that the giant keeper had trained to do. Shot-stopping and claiming high balls? Yes. Smiling, laughing and generally having a good time? No. Torstooper was still very confused by a son he didn't know he had turning up and eating his *Apfelstrudel*. Learning that his former girlfriend, whom he hadn't spoken to in nearly thirteen years, was also at the World Cup was also very confusing. He shook his head and tried to flick his brain back into football mode.

Coren didn't seem that convinced by Cairo's reasoning, but he let it rest for now. He hadn't brushed his hair up and back, up and back, for over ten minutes now, and it was starting to flop down. He was a very short man, and his hair was very important to him; it made him feel much taller than he actually was.

'You are a short, fat, arrogant, self-absorbed idiot,' said Prussia to Coren, switching to German so he wouldn't understand him. Beware when someone you know suddenly starts talking in a foreign language. It usually means they are talking about you.

Coren looked at Torstooper for a translation.

'He said he is really looking forward to continuing to work with you and Torstooper to win the World Cup.'

'Well, that's nice,' said Coren with a smile. 'I'm looking forward to it, too.'

27
TACTICAL DECISIONS

The mighty Brazil would be waiting for England in the quarter-finals of the World Cup. Brazil were renowned as one of the best attacking teams in the world. Even their goalkeeper, Silko, liked to take shots at goal. He was currently the world's top-scoring goalkeeper, with seven international goals, which was seven more than most of the England team. He took free kicks, penalties and throw-ins, presented the weather on Brazilian TV, and sometimes played the clarinet in the Rio de Janeiro Symphony Orchestra. The last thing a manager and teammates want in a goalkeeper is unpredictability, and Silko had it by the bucket-load.

Tim sat in the breakfast room at the hotel, studying the Brazilian team and their tactics, scribbling in his little black notepad. This is what joint England head coaches had to do. He knew Silko was the Achilles heel of the team if you got him on one of his bad days. Get him on one of his good days, and he would probably save two penalties, and blast home the winner at the same time.

This was a tough job for Tim. McCloud was concentrating on blending the llamas and professional human footballers into the perfect team. Which wasn't easy when only eight of them wanted to train. Greg Punch's mob were camped out by the pool refusing to take part. There was one bit of positive news: Sid Melonhead had joined McCloud's group, following his winning goal against Japan. He had started to form a great bond with Lightning, and regularly practised sprinting with her, which she loved.

Even though Tim's family had arrived to support him in Mucho Plata, they weren't much help managing an international football team. Fiona spent most of her time on what she called 'special-op missions'. Monica was totally engrossed in social media for both Llama United and the England team, and she'd done a great job – all the woe and misery from the group stages had been washed away, and now the fans were full of positivity and encouragement. Frank and Beetroot were treating the trip to Mucho Plata as a holiday. It was the first proper break they'd had in ages, and they were loving it. Their day consisted of discussing what food to eat and what they should have to drink. Who would have thought two people could have such long conversations about the style of chip served at the all-day buffet?

It was Cairo's mum, Molly, who got the really tough job: trying to keep the seven 'holiday llamas' in check without Cairo. He would return from the Germany camp late in the evening, with just enough time to wish his mum goodnight before he went to sleep. Then, first thing in the morning, he would dash off to spend time with his dad. He didn't seem to want to talk to her about it, and Molly was very worried, but she was so busy looking for wandering 'holiday llamas', she didn't have a great deal of time for chatting.

Dasher enjoyed swimming in the pool. The hotel guests didn't enjoy her swimming in the pool. Bob had somehow convinced the hotel barber to give him regular daily haircuts, which is impressive, considering Bob doesn't speak human. The Duke visited the local shopping mall, and acquired a top hat, three very smart bow ties and a gold-handled walking cane. No, I don't know how he did this, either. Barcelona had found the hotel nightclub and spent most of the day and evening learning new dance moves. He got very good at the shuffle, popping and locking, and some freezes. Bill and Brian finally broke into the chocolate mousse barn and had a dip in one of the huge vats of chocolate. Chocolate mousse on Mucho Plata tasted a bit llama-y for at least a week after that. Smasher didn't do anything. As I've already told you, he doesn't like to make a fuss.

Tim and Cairo had hardly spoken since the day Cairo left to find his dad. Tim spent most of his time on the training pitch, and Cairo at the German camp, so their paths rarely crossed. Molly had told Tim about what was happening, but somehow it only pushed the best friends further apart. Tim couldn't believe that Cairo would just ignore the England World Cup preparations so easily. Surely he could speak to his dad after the tournament had finished? Cairo hardly knew anything about Torstooper, a man who Tim knew had devoted his life to football and nothing else, shunning everything – and everyone – in the pursuit of becoming an all-time football great. Why would Torstooper suddenly change this plan and start being bothered about a son he had shown no interest in before? It didn't make sense.

Then Tim started getting suspicious. Maybe Cairo was passing on their tactics to his dad to impress him? No, surely he wouldn't do that . . . He *was* still his best friend, wasn't he? Besides, Tim never let his little black tactics notepad out of his sight, even when he was in the shower.

Tim had to put Cairo to the back of his mind for now, and focus on the Brazil match. He could only select players he knew his four llamas could trust: the ones in McCloud's group, not Punch's. It wasn't ideal, as Punch had a few players he could really use, like Jim Hoisin, who had the potential to win games on his own. He looked at his skeleton team for the clash with Brazil. He had enough to field a starting eleven, in a 4-4-1-1 formation, but didn't have any subs.

Ludo

T. J. Wilkinson   Melonhead   Useless   Brussell

Lightning   Cruncher   Tart   Steakhouse (c)

Tablecloth

Goal Machine
Subs: None

International management wasn't as much fun as managing a team of llamas in the Cup. Tim looked out of the window towards the training pitch. McCloud stood in the centre circle, waving his arms about. The England players and the llamas were practising free kicks over a wall made up of Frank, Beetroot and Monica, none of whom was happy about this. Frank had already been hit three times in the stomach by Cruncher's wayward efforts. Motorway stood off behind the goal with Fiona, who was brushing the knots out of her wool and putting a huge gold bow on top of her head. As the so-called princesses of the team, they didn't get involved with training. Motorway eyed herself in the mirror Fiona had provided and nodded her approval. The Brazil match would be her first of the tournament, and she wanted to look her best for the thousands of fans who had come to see her in action.

The England players burst into applause. Goal Machine had just put an absolute screamer of a free kick into the top right-hand corner of the net. Tim smiled. They'd need that kind of magic in the quarter-final. Could his team deliver? The weight of the whole country was now on Tim's shoulders. They *had* to beat Brazil.

28
WORLD CUP QUARTER-FINAL: ENGLAND V BRAZIL

The two teams took the field, Brazil in their famous yellow shirts and England in their red away kit. Tim could see that Silko, the Brazilian goalkeeper, was pumped up for the match. Almost too pumped up. He was leaping up and down like a jack-in-the-box as the national anthems were sung, and hollering and shouting orders at his teammates. He hugged each player individually before the start of the match, then went round the England team and did exactly the same. Even the llamas got a hug, which none of them enjoyed – especially Cruncher, who was already anxiously nibbling his own shirt: he didn't like the colour red.

As the ref peeped his whistle to get the game under way, Tim noticed that Silko had taken his starting position way outside his own penalty area, which was unusual. This was going to be an interesting match.

Brazil won their first free kick after just eight minutes, when Chaz Steakhouse clumsily brought down the Brazilian right back, Moodo. Silko casually stepped up to take it, even though it was deep inside the England half. The entire Brazilian team went into the England area to receive the ball. This left the whole Brazilian half of the pitch and their goal totally empty of players. The Brazil manager didn't seem to be bothered in the slightest.

McCloud stood next to Tim. 'Big opportunities here, Tim – counter-attack will be the key,' he said, with his hand over his mouth so the people watching on TV couldn't lip-read what he was saying.

Silko began his run-up from his own half and charged at the ball as fast as he possibly could.

'Ach, he'll never make it from there,' scoffed McCloud.

'CRAACCKKKKKKK,' screamed the ball, as Silko's right foot smashed into it. The ball soared like a missile, wobbling slightly left and right in the hot afternoon air. The England and Brazil players in the area just stood and admired it as it zoomed in on the top right-hand corner of the goal. Tim winced and shut his eyes . . . It was going in!

Silko turned and lifted his arms towards the baying

sea of yellow Brazil fans behind the goal.

'Ach, Bhoys, Terrors, Blue Brazil and Spiders!' shouted McCloud in his own unique form of swearing. That's a lot of swear words, even for McCloud.

Even the ref was about to blow his whistle for a goal: probably the longest long-range goal in the history of the World Cup . . .

Then from nowhere a hairy black blur flew across the goal. It was Ludo. Just as the ball was about to fly into the corner of the net, as if in slow motion, the smallest, shortest tongue you have ever seen poked itself out of Ludo's mouth and flicked the ball over the bar. What a save!

The England fans took over the cheers from the Brazil fans and started chanting, 'LUDO, LUDO, LUDO, LUDO.' Their song-making skills hadn't improved since the last game.

Both Tim and McCloud said some positive words of encouragement to the team in the changing room at half-time. They all knew that the game couldn't remain at 0 – 0 for much longer: it was too open. England had to be the team to strike first.

In the fifty-second minute, Brazil won a free kick on the edge of the centre circle. Silko hoofed the ball incredibly high into the air. When it came down from the sky, it had reached the edge of the England area, where a Brazilian midfielder headed it back high into the air. This was a very unusual strategy.

'I dinnae like this,' muttered McCloud.

'Look, it's Silko!' shouted Tim, pointing at the Brazilian keeper sprinting up the pitch. He was wearing pink, so was easy to pick out.

The Brazilian keeper had charged from where he took the free kick all the way into the area, and before you could say 'Oi, someone clear it!' he had risen acrobatically to bicycle-kick the ball into the back of the England net. Ludo didn't stand a chance. What a finish, and from his own free kick!

BRAZIL 1 – 0 ENGLAND

Silko didn't shy away from celebrating his incredible goal. He ran three laps of the pitch, blowing kisses to everyone in the ground, then he and the rest of the Brazilian team did an elaborate samba dance in the centre circle that went on for at least five minutes.

Tim slumped back into his chair in the dugout.

'Plenty of time, laddie, dinnae you worry,' said McCloud. 'Just a blip.'

McCloud was right. In the sixty-first minute Silko started arrogantly juggling the ball on the edge of his own area, flicking it between his feet and up on top of his head, where he balanced it for a few minutes, to the cheers of the Brazilian crowd.

Cruncher had taken as much as a llama could take of this ridiculous show, especially as he hadn't touched the ball in the last ten minutes. Which is a long time for a llama. He slowly started jogging up from his position in midfield. This soon became a trot, then a canter, and then a full-on sprint. Silko was too busy entertaining the crowd to notice the llama running at him full tilt. Before he had time to gather the ball safely in his arms, Cruncher had nodded the ball off the top of his head and into the gaping wide-open net.

ENGLAND 1 – 1 BRAZIL!

Cruncher had a little nibble on the corner of Silko's long shorts by way of celebration. Tim and McCloud danced a little jig on the side of the pitch. It felt like the old days of their cup run, except without Cairo.

'Ah told you, laddie, it was just a blip. We are going to stroll home, just you watch,' McCloud said excitedly.

McCloud was right again. Silko was determined to make up for his mistake. He started to go on longer and longer mazy dribbles with the ball. He beat three

England players, before he was eventually tackled by Chaz Steakhouse, leaving his goal dangerously exposed. In less time than it takes to eat three salt and vinegar crisps, Steakhouse had passed to Tablecloth, who found Goal Machine with a beautiful through ball. All Goal Machine had to do was roll the ball into an open net. He casually lowered his neck and knocked the ball in with his head.

ENGLAND 2 – 1 BRAZIL!

The England crowd went berserk. They were just ten minutes from a World Cup semi-final, a place they hadn't been for a very, very, very, very, very long time. Ask your dad, or maybe even your granddad. England were not done. Melonhead added his second in two games from ten yards out, and in the last minute of the match, Goal Machine cracked in the fourth from a free kick, just like he'd done in training.

Final score:

ENGLAND 4 – 1 BRAZIL

WOW!!!

The yellow samba party behind the goal had all gone home. It was England who would be celebrating long into the night, with Argentina waiting for them in the semi-final. Tim felt a massive weight lift from his shoulders as the players left the pitch following their celebrations. He would finally get a good night's sleep for the first time in ages. He gave Ludo, Goal Machine and Cruncher congratulatory hugs as they trotted off the turf. Lightning was a bit further behind . . .

She was limping!

29
LIMPING LIGHTNING

Back at the hotel, Molly inspected Lightning's four legs. Every time she went near the right-side hind leg, Lightning would jolt away and make an angry hissing noise.

'She won't let me get anywhere near that back leg,' said Molly, wiping her muddy hands on her white England tracksuit. 'I've got no idea what's up. It could be ligament damage, a strain, a bruise, or just something caught in between her toes.'

'Why dunnae we hold her down so you can get a proper look at her?' suggested McCloud.

'We could give it a try, I suppose,' said Molly. 'Won't be easy though. Tim, you and I will distract her from the front, and McCloud, you come round the back.'

McCloud nodded, spat into his hands and rubbed them together.

'OK, after three,' called Molly, holding up her hand. 'One, two, thr—'

She didn't have time to finish her words. McCloud lurched forward too early and swiftly clamped both his hands on Lightning's back.

'No, McCloud, too early!' shouted Molly, leaping into action, quickly followed by Tim.

Lightning liked McCloud grabbing her back leg as much as she did snot-flavoured ice cream. Not at all.

Her head swung round and she let out an unusual panicked howl. Her good left hind leg lifted hastily and unceremoniously lashed out towards McCloud, catching him squarely between the legs.

'OOOOOOFFFFFFFFFF.'

Tim closed his eyes and winced. McCloud stood stock-still, as though he had been frozen on the spot by a special super-hero freeze-ray gun. Molly, Tim and even Lightning stopped everything and watched.

McCloud's face began to slowly go purple. Then he toppled to the ground like a huge Scots pine tree being felled in a forest, both his hands clamped firmly between his legs.

'STENNY, GABLE ENDIES, SHIRE, FIFERS, BINOS, TON, LOONS, JAGS, BUDDIES, ACCIES, KILLIES, HIBEES, DONS AND THE SOONS!!!' bellowed McCloud at the top of his voice while he rolled around on the floor. Now that *is* a lot of swearing for McCloud.

Molly, Tim and Lightning watched him do this for what seemed like twenty minutes. Molly and Tim tried to make comforting 'Oooh, poor you' noises, but sadly, that never helps.

Eventually McCloud got back to his feet. Took a deep lungful of muggy Mucho Plata air. Stretched his arms out. And then clapped his hands together. 'So where were we?' he said, as though nothing had happened.

'I don't think Lightning will let the three of us

inspect her,' said Molly, shaking her head slowly.

Tim slumped to the floor, cupped his head in his hands, and let out a puff of exasperated air. 'Why does this always happen to us, McCloud?' he said mournfully. 'Why can't anything be easy, for just one game?'

'This is fitba', laddie. Nothing is ever simple in fitba',' he said, wincing as he laughed. 'I've played hundreds of games for different clubs and at international level, and it's always like this. Hurdle after hurdle after hurdle. I'm surprised footballers don't become Olympic hurdlers. Fitba' would be very boring without all this background shenanigans.'

'I hate it,' said Tim. 'I just want to play and win matches.'

'So do I, laddie, so do I.' McCloud put a hand on Tim's shoulder and began patting it. This felt very unusual. McCloud wasn't great with sympathy. But at least he was trying.

'You know who could help us solve the Lightning problem?' said Molly, wiping more mud on to her tracksuit.

'Who?' replied Tim. He knew what Molly was going to say next. He just didn't want to admit it to himself.

'Cairo.'

30
MEETING THE
GOLDEN OCTOPUS

Molly was right: the llamas – and England – needed Cairo. Now they were being selected for the team, they needed him more than ever. He had a magic touch. He knew all their physical quirks better than anyone. Molly was great with most animals, but when it came to Llama United, they only really trusted Cairo. Lightning would definitely let him look at her injury.

Tim didn't think ringing Cairo was the best way to patch up their friendship. He had to get into the German training camp where Cairo spent nearly all his time now. Which wouldn't be easy for the England head coach. I mean, you can't just stroll up and knock on the front door.

It was time to call on Fiona . . . again. She's turned into quite a useful sister to have, hasn't she?

And it was Fiona who managed to smuggle Tim

into the German base dressed as a techno DJ. If I had any idea what this music actually is, I'd explain it a bit more. I've just about got to grips with rock 'n' roll. Which might have something to do with sandwiches, I think.

Anyway, Fiona dressed Tim in white jeans and a white T-shirt, put bright green sweatbands around his wrists, and gave him large shades and a bright pink baseball cap. She topped off the disguise with a huge moustache and a mullet attached to the back of Tim's hair. She gave him two huge metal record cases to carry, and another DJ satchel to sling over his shoulder. This seemed like a lot of fuss just to have a quick chat with Cairo, but Fiona was very insistent that it wouldn't work without it.

She then put Tim into a huge laundry basket outside the hotel, and let their staff unknowingly wheel it into the depths of the hotel. Tim pointed out that he didn't need the disguise if he was just going in via the laundry basket, but Fiona was again very insistent and she waved her fist at him. So Tim shut up.

Once inside the hotel, it took Tim ages to find Cairo's room. Mainly because he got asked to play a DJ set in the hotel nightclub. That lasted two hours.

He went down very well and was asked to perform again in a week's time. All he did was play the same record over and over again.

He left the hotel nightclub and continued his hunt. Fiona's detailed information dossier on the German hotel revealed that Cairo was in room 1966. Which apparently has a significant meaning, for some reason.

When he got to the door, he suddenly felt incredibly nervous and could feel some sick bubbling up in the pit of his stomach.

'Come on,' he told himself under his breath. 'This is Cairo, your best friend, your only proper friend. Well, the only one with two legs, anyway.'

Tim didn't have time to knock. The door was opened slowly by a round man with a white beard and a boater hat. He was dressed like one of those gondola drivers in Venice. It was Heinrich Prussia.

Tim didn't have time to speak. The man turned his head and began barking German back into the room. Tim didn't have a clue what he was talking about, so let me translate. (I'm getting quite good at this.)

'There is a techno DJ at the door. He was talking to himself. If he didn't have a fabulous moustache and that brilliant haircut, I'd say he looked exactly like that England llama boy.'

Torstooper appeared behind Prussia, in a tiny black-and-white-striped towel.

'Why have you knocked on Torstooper's door?' said Torstooper robotically, seeing through Tim's feeble disguise straight away. 'Torstooper is unhappy that you are not actually a techno DJ. Torstooper is a fan of techno.'

'Erm, technically I didn't knock,' said Tim nervily. 'This man opened the door.'

'Torstooper will repeat the question,' said Torstooper. 'Why have you knocked on Torstooper's door?'

'I wanted to speak to Cairo,' said Tim. 'Is he there, please?'

'This is very unlikely,' said Torstooper. 'Torstooper's son is not very happy with you. However, you may come in to see how great

197

Torstooper's son has it now. Follow Torstooper.'

The Golden Octopus escorted Tim into his opulent penthouse suite. It was much more impressive than Tim's tiny room back at the England hotel. There was a huge lounge with three enormous sofas, with more cushions than you would ever need. Off the lounge was a small kitchen, and two gigantic bedrooms with treble-sized giant emperor mattresses. Both bedrooms were en-suite and had individual showers, baths, plunge pools and saunas. Tim tried to take in the surroundings but he was mainly concerned about Torstooper's towel falling off as he walked along behind him.

Cairo was sitting in a gaming chair facing a huge TV, playing on a golden games console. He had two huge milkshakes next to him – one butterscotch, the other raspberry – and a pile of sweets that would take at least a day to get through. He was wearing a branded Torstooper green goalkeeping kit, with a big '1' on the back and a golden octopus on the front. Cairo glanced over his shoulder. 'Oh, it's you,' he said glumly, returning his eyes to the TV screen.

Torstooper and Prussia took up positions as close as possible to Cairo, like they were huge guard dogs. This made Tim feel even more uncomfortable.

'I wanted to speak to you, Cairo,' said Tim, clearing his throat. He could feel the sweat building on his back again.

Cairo paused his game and sighed. 'Come to brag about how you've become England manager and how you managed to beat Japan and Brazil?' he said meanly.

'Er, no, not really,' replied Tim. His heart fluttered slightly that Cairo had at least been interested enough to check the scores.

'I'm having a great time with my dad,' said Cairo defiantly, waggling his butterscotch milkshake at Tim. 'I've got everything I could ever want. It's so nice having a brilliant dad like mine and not having to think about football all the time. Like with you.'

'You don't talk about football at *all* here?' asked Tim, slightly surprised.

Cairo looked at the two Germans flanking him, and started to get a little flustered. 'Well, of course we talk about football but . . . erm . . . that's normal when your dad is a famous player. But we also talk about other things, too.'

'Like what?'

'Erm . . . well, erm . . .' replied Cairo. He started concentrating on the straw in his milkshake.

'Milkshakes and, erm . . . their different flavours.'

Tim screwed up his face; he wasn't convinced that Cairo was having a better time here, apart from the free milkshakes. Tim changed the subject. Cairo was being so pig-headed, it was making him forget that he was trying to get Cairo's help. 'You know you can't start supporting the German team just because of your dad,' he said foolishly. 'You are part of the England team – you support them.'

'Why, what's wrong with spending time with the German team and supporting England too?' replied Cairo defensively.

Tim cackled. 'Everyone knows you can't support two teams. That's like the worst thing ever.'

'Why is it the worst thing ever?' Cairo's voice was getting steadily angrier each time he spoke.

'Because it is. You can only choose one team and you have to stick with them for life. It's a basic rule of being a football supporter.'

'Nobody has ever told me that. Seems like a silly rule to me,' said Cairo.

'That's because you don't concentrate on the football world around you. All this stuff is really important.'

'Well, it's not *that* important. Look what football

has done to *my* family,' shouted Cairo, waving both his hands in the air. 'It's not as important as being with your family. Don't you agree, Dad?' asked Cairo. 'Spending time with your son is much more important than choosing which football team to support?'

Torstooper remained silent, then Prussia applied a subtle dig of his elbow into the Golden Octopus's ribs. 'Yeerrsss,' he said unconvincingly. 'Whatever Torstooper's son just said is correct.'

Tim took a step back, as though he'd been punched in the stomach. Was Cairo turning his back on England and now supporting Germany because of his dad? Tim had come to make peace, and now Cairo had made him angry again. Maybe mentioning the Lightning injury might make Cairo change his mind.

'So you don't care about the llamas either, now that you are with Germany?' questioned Tim.

'Of course I care about the llamas,' replied Cairo shortly. 'Nothing will stop me caring about them. But with Mum around, I know they're in safe hands, so I could come and spend time with my dad. He'll be going back to Germany after this, and I won't get to see him as much.'

'They really miss you, and Lightning is injured. We need your llama-healing skills,' said Tim.

'Lightning is injured?' Cairo sat up and put down his milkshake, looking worried.

'She has a damaged back leg,' continued Tim. 'I'm worried that she'll miss the semi-final against Argentina.'

Cairo went quiet. Heinrich Prussia started shifting uneasily about in his seat again. The silence was deafening.

'Is that all you care about? Lightning missing the semi-final?' asked Cairo, looking out the window. 'Or are you actually worried about Lightning?'

'Erm, well I . . . erm . . . didn't mean it like that,' replied Tim, floundering. 'But it's not just a match – this is the World Cup. It's the most important thing ever.' Tim paused and put his other foot in it by saying something incredibly stupid. The stupidest thing a boy could ever say to his best friend. 'You need to choose right now: England or Germany.'

At first Cairo didn't reply. He kept looking out the window, trying to keep a lid on the raging fire of anger in his tummy.

'*Why* do I have to choose?' he hissed eventually, through gritted teeth.

'Because you have to. You clearly don't care about us, or the llamas. Choose.'

'Well, in that case I choose Germany,' said Cairo, folding his arms angrily and turning away from Tim.

'So you're turning your back on me and the llamas,' Tim said, his voice rising.

'I don't want to, but you're forcing me. You don't care about anything apart from football.'

'It's the World Cup!' shouted Tim. 'THE WORLD CUP.'

'I DON'T CARE ABOUT THE WORLD CUP,' shouted Cairo, right into Tim's face.

Torstooper stepped in between Tim and Cairo before it got any angrier, and moved them apart, offering his son some calming words as he led him away.

'It is time you should be going now,' said Prussia. 'You have outstayed your welcome.'

He got up and started ushering Tim out the room with the end of his walking stick. Tim retreated from the room, his body trembling all over with rage and his fists crunched into two tight balls of fury. Prussia was surprisingly light on his feet for an old man with a walking stick, and in seconds Tim found himself shepherded back into the hotel corridor and the room door slammed in his face.

31
THE CAIRO PLOT

Back in the room, Cairo was sitting in one of the very comfy armchairs trying to calm himself down. Torstooper had placed a cold, wet flannel over Cairo's face. It wasn't helping at all, and was beginning to drip on to his shoulders.

'So that boy and you are good friends?' asked Prussia, with a chuckle, as he returned to the sofas.

'We were,' said Cairo glumly, from under the flannel. He still couldn't believe how the World Cup had managed to tear the two of them apart. Before the tournament Tim and Cairo had been inseparable.

'But you have us now,' said Prussia, with a false, toothy smile.

'I've had a lovely time here,' said Cairo, taking a deep breath, 'but I'm beginning to think I should go back and at least check on the llamas. Lightning is injured, after all.'

Prussia went white and wrinkled his nose in disgust.

'It has been a stressful day,' he said. 'I think that it is dangerous if you go back to the hotel and see Tim. It might damage your friendship forever,' he added carefully, 'and you wouldn't want that, would you?'

Cairo shook his head solemnly. Perhaps some time away from the England camp was a good idea. It might give both of them time to cool down.

'Why don't you have a lie-down in the other room, and you can ring your mother and tell her the news after you have had a sleep?'

'Yes, I am a bit tired, I suppose,' said Cairo removing the flannel from his face. 'I think I will close my eyes for a bit . . .' Cairo hauled himself out of the comfy armchair and disappeared into one of the rooms.

Prussia waited a few seconds to check that Cairo had gone, then began babbling urgently in German to Torstooper.

'We can't let him go back to the llamas and the England team,' said Prussia. 'It will ruin my plan.'

'What plan?' replied Torstooper. 'This is the first time you have mentioned a plan to Torstooper.'

'Remember when you were a young goalkeeper over in England? I saved you from a lifetime of misery and toil in the worst leagues in the world.'

Torstooper nodded.

'I brought you back to Germany and trained you up,' continued Prussia. 'I turned you from a weakling into strong German iron. In three years you became the best goalkeeper in the world. You have won everything . . . and it's all down to me. You are called the Golden Octopus because of me.'

'It is true, you did give Torstooper an amazing career,' added Torstooper.

'This boy sitting here in the bedroom is your flesh and blood,' continued Prussia. 'Now it is time I – *we* – saved him from his miserable life with the England team and those animals, and made him great, like you. It can be your legacy.'

'I am not sure he would want that,' said Torstooper thoughtfully. 'He likes those animals. They seem very important to him. I wouldn't want to see him upset because he missed them.'

'Pfftttt . . . Have you gone soft all of a sudden?' Prussia snorted. 'Every boy wants this dream.

Becoming a world–class player, taking over from his father in the German goal. Becoming a legend. Being rich . . .'

'Perhaps we should ask him if he wants this,' said Torstooper, getting up to go and retrieve Cairo from the bedroom.

Prussia grabbed Torstooper's huge knee, pinched his fingers together over his lips, and guided him back to his seat.

'No, we can't tell him the plan just yet,' whispered Prussia. 'We cannot have any distractions, what with the World Cup final coming up. Distractions ruin great players.'

'Is this why you convinced me to leave England?' said Torstooper coldly. 'Too many distractions?'

Prussia blushed and began furiously shaking his head. 'No, no, no, of course not . . . of course not,' he babbled, rubbing his hands together.

Torstooper paused and stared deeply into Prussia's cold, grey eyes. Prussia blinked several times and his mouth began twitching.

'It is OK, Torstooper believes you,' said Torstooper at last, like a fool. 'You can train my boy after Torstooper wins the World Cup with Germany.'

'Excellent,' replied Prussia, secretly rubbing his fingers together by his side.

Training up another world-class goalkeeper meant one thing to him: money, and lots of it.

32
THE HEIST

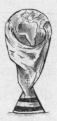

As we all know, England's biggest rivals in international football are the Germans. However, following very close behind them is Argentina. For Greg Punch and his team of exiles, there was very little to be happy about. England had easily qualified for the semi-final with Argentina with just eleven players. Punch's silly rebellion was being mocked in the media and it was making him angrier and angrier. *He* was England's captain, an England legend. But everything he had done in the past was being forgotten. The media were now all in love with Cruncher, his hairy replacement in the team.

Punch's band of followers were also starting to split up. He'd already lost Melonhead, and now five other players had apologized and returned to the main squad with Tim and McCloud. The rebels now numbered just six – Punch, Badger, Peacock, Hoisin,

Cheeks and Hussain-Bolt – all Nork Town players.

Punch was also getting incredibly annoyed with the so-called 'holiday llamas', who were still causing chaos around the hotel, but unintentionally appeared to have focused their efforts on Punch and his henchmen. Bill and Brian had taken to leaving large piles of poo outside their rooms. Dasher liked splashing the players by doing huge bombs into the pool. Barcelona would block the door to the nightclub and bar so they couldn't get in. Bob would spit in their soup when they weren't looking, and the Duke kept stealing their mobile phones. Smasher didn't do anything. I've told you already: he doesn't like to make a fuss.

Poor Molly was constantly chasing them out of the hotel and pool area. It was exhausting. She had no one to help her. McCloud and Tim were always training. Cairo was so wrapped up with his visits to the German camp, he was now having sleepovers there. She felt guilty about asking Frank and Beetroot as they were enjoying their holiday so much. Monica spent most of her time on her laptop. And Fiona? Who knew what she was getting up to? Sweet-smuggling?

Punch didn't want to be left out of England's game with Argentina. But he wasn't the type of person to apologize, especially to a twelve-year-old. There had to be another way of getting into the team. He just needed to remove the only player in the team who was in his position – Cruncher. As he lay on his sun-lounger watching the rest of the England team training for the semi-final, he came up with a plan. A plan only someone like Greg Punch could think of, because he wasn't actually a very nice person. But you should have worked that out for yourself already . . .

Later that evening, the England captain slipped into the llama stables and coaxed Cruncher towards the huge shopping mall across the road, using an incredibly delicious five-tier chocolate cake. Close your eyes and think of the best-looking cake ever . . . Now throw a load of sprinkles, chocolate buttons, marshmallows and salted caramel sauce on it . . . Then smear it in chocolate mousse. Now you have Greg Punch's cake.

Once inside the shopping mall, and after the cake had been devoured, Punch looped a handbag over Cruncher's neck and dragged him into a huge and expensive jewellery shop. Mucho Plata was full of expensive jewellery shops. Once there, Punch carefully and secretly loaded the handbag with gold watches, diamond rings and silver necklaces. Then Punch just walked out of the shop, leaving Cruncher behind with the handbag full of loot.

Now this was the clever bit (sort of) to Punch's plan: he knew that Cruncher would eventually get bored of just standing around in a jewellery shop and would soon leave of his own free will, probably to look for something else to eat. Once he left the shopping mall, the alarms would go off and he would

be arrested for theft. Punch was so confident that this would happen, he went back to the hotel, got into bed and went to sleep. Yes, I know. He forgot to clean his teeth.

Half an hour later, Punch was woken by the sound of screaming sirens from across the road. It looked like the entire Mucho Plata police force had descended on the shopping mall. To be honest, they didn't have a lot to do. Cruncher stood outside, totally oblivious to what was going on, watching the flashing blue lights of the police cars and wagons fill up the street.

Next thing he knew, he was in the back of a police van, being taken to a prison cell.

33
BREAKING BAD NEWS

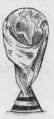

Tim stood in the transporter van as Molly led the llamas and Motorway into their places for the short trip to the Golden Nugget Stadium for the clash with Argentina. She hadn't noticed she only had ten llamas. Tim was in a bit of a trance. His nerves had been getting worse the closer they got to the Cup final. All he could think about was trying to stop his breakfast exploding all over the floor, even though he hadn't actually had any breakfast. He'd been in the toilet since he got up.

He was also coming to terms with not being able to pick Lightning. She hadn't recovered from her injury, and with Cairo unlikely to return any time soon, she was going to miss the semi-final and was a big doubt for the final – if England even made it that far.

'You OK, Tim?' asked Molly, giving him one of

her best smiles. 'It'll all be over soon, don't worry.' Then she realized what she had said. 'I mean, not like that, not like getting-knocked-out-today "over soon". Ooooh . . . I should just keep quiet, sorry . . .'

She went back to busying herself with the llamas. The 'holiday llamas' weren't fans of going to matches they weren't playing in, so kept trying to escape.

McCloud walked briskly up to the transporter. His face looked pained, as though he had several tiny annoying stones in his socks. 'OK, laddie, dunnae get worried now, but we've got a problem,' he said as calmly as he could. 'Cruncher has been arrested for jewellery theft.'

Tim stared blankly at McCloud as the information leaked into his brain. Then he laughed, a deep hearty laugh that went on for a good few seconds. He hadn't laughed like this in ages.

McCloud glared at him.

'This is nae laughing matter,' he said. 'He's in a holding cell at Mucho Plata jail. Awaiting trial.'

Tim burst out laughing again. 'Oh, McCloud, you could have come up with something better! That's ridiculous, but I suppose it's done the trick. I do feel much better. Laughter is good for you.'

McCloud continued to stare at Tim. He scratched

the tip of his nose, and flicked away what could have been a small bogey. 'This is nae prank, laddie,' he said, without a flicker of cheer. 'This is deadly serious.'

Tim smirked and then his face dropped. 'Wait? What, really?'

McCloud nodded solemnly again. 'Aye, really, really.'

A tiny two-seater car screeched up alongside the transporter. Frank was driving, and a small figure dressed in black was in the passenger seat holding a bright pink smoothie.

'Don't worry,' shouted the small figure, taking a slurp of her drink. It was Fiona. 'We're going down to the jail now to break Cruncher free.'

Frank rolled his eyes. 'No we're not.'

'Break Cruncher free?' asked Tim.

'Yes, I'm going to save him from jail, using my ninja stealth skills,' she said, tapping her nose secretively.

'This is serious, FIONA,' shouted Tim. 'Let me get in the car. You are not the right person for this.'

'I am so!!!' barked Fiona.

'You are not.'

'I am. Infinity million and no comebacks.' Fiona stuck out her tongue for good measure.

'Will you both stop!' came a muffled voice from

the boot of the car. The door flipped open, and there, folded inside, was Monica and her trusty computer.

'Don't worry, Tim,' she said. 'I'll sort this out in no time. Just go along with Fiona – it's much easier for all of us if we do. We'll be back before the semifinal starts, I promise.'

'But how?' pleaded Tim.

'It involves the use of these,' said Monica, holding up both her hands and waving them in the air, which made the many bracelets on her wrists rattle and crack together.

Tim was confused.

'Let's roll, Dad,' she called, slamming the boot shut.

Frank pushed his foot down on the accelerator, and within seconds they were gone.

34
LLAMA LIBERATION

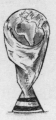

The Mucho Plata jail was incredibly posh. So posh, it was mainly used as a tourist destination since it was made out of solid gold, which isn't the greatest construction material because it makes everything so slippery. Prison guards were constantly falling over as they led inmates to their cells or served them food. Not that Mucho Plata had many prisoners. It was a holiday island and most people were there to have fun. In fact, apart from Cruncher, Mucho Plata had only ever had one other prisoner. He was called Jeff Christmas. You won't be surprised to hear he was a burglar who specialized in entering and leaving people's houses through the chimney. He was caught every time.

The jail was surrounded by the Press and TV camera crews when the Gravy car arrived. So many that Frank had to park three streets away and stay in the car because there were loads of his ultimate enemy, the traffic warden, stalking the place. Fiona and Monica leaped out of the car and battled their way through the crowds.

'I'll go round the back!' shouted Fiona, disappearing off before Monica had a chance to stop her.

Monica knocked on a small golden shutter on the front door of the jail.

'No Press or TV,' snapped a voice from inside.

'I'm not Press or TV,' replied Monica calmly. 'I'm Monica Gravy. We own Cruncher the llama.'

The shutter opened cautiously and a pair of eyes looked Monica suspiciously up and down.

'You don't look like a llama owner,' said the man behind the door.

'What is a llama owner supposed to look like?' asked Monica. 'If you let me in I will guarantee that this crowd of people will be gone in the next half an hour, and you can go back to being a tourist spot.'

The shutter slammed closed and she could hear mutterings from the other side of the door. Then a stronger-sounding voice joined the muttering one, shouting in a language Monica didn't understand. Within seconds the sound of bolts slamming sideways and keys jangling in locks started, and eventually the heavy door swept open. A tall man, impeccably dressed in a smart red military uniform stood in the hallway of the jail.

'I apologize for my corporal,' said the smart soldier, giving a little bow. 'Captain Kneeslide, at your service. I have just arrived back from seeing my mother. She has not been well. Too much chocolate mousse . . . So I come back to find my jailhouse surrounded by TV people, which is not good for the tourists, and rumours of a llama in one of the cells.'

'He's been wrongly arrested,' said Monica dramatically, 'for jewellery theft.'

'Ah, I see,' said Captain Kneeslide, stroking his chin. 'Can you prove the llama didn't do it?'

'Quite easily,' replied Monica. She raised her hands. 'How does a llama steal jewellery from a shop when he doesn't have any fingers or thumbs?'

Jeff Christmas was annoying Cruncher. The burglar was making neighing, horsey noises at the llama from the other side of the cell corridor. Cruncher couldn't understand what this man covered in soot was saying, but it was getting on his nerves.

SCRAPE, SCRAPE, SCRAPE, SCRAPE, came a noise from the barred window of Cruncher's cell.

Fiona's head popped up.

'I'm getting you out, Cruncher. Sit . . . er, stand tight. We'll be through here in a jiffy.'

SCRAPE, SCRAPE, SCRAPE, SCRAPE. She continued filing at the bars in the cell window with a soup spoon she had borrowed from the hotel. As you know, soup spoons hate being used for anything other than soup, cereals or puddings, so it was refusing to help.

'Oi, get me out too,' whined Jeff Christmas. 'I'll be good, I promise.'

Suddenly the main door swung open, and Captain Kneeslide strode into the room. Monica walked behind him. The jail guard leaped up from his seat and saluted the captain.

'Captain Kneeslide,' said the flustered guard, standing to attention. 'I didn't expect you to be coming into the jail today, CAPTAIN.'

'Why is this llama locked up in my prison?' asked Captain Kneeslide.

'He stole around three million dollars' worth of jewellery last night from the shopping mall, CAPTAIN,' replied the guard, in a shouty, soldiery kind of way.

'And how did he do that?'

'He put them in a large handbag and walked out of the shop, CAPTAIN.'

The captain loomed in closely towards the guard's face. 'And can you explain to me how a llama, who doesn't have hands, carefully places jewellery into a handbag, zips it closed and buttons down a flap?'

Monica smiled broadly. As expected, it hadn't taken long to convince the captain, especially as he didn't want her blabbing to the media that they had wrongly locked up a World Cup star.

'Erm . . . erm . . . erm,' said the guard, racking his brain for an answer. 'He used his mouth?' He beamed a wide grin. That seemed like a good answer.

'This llama eats everything that goes near his mouth, and what would a llama do with loads of jewellery anyway?'

'Birthday presents?' squeaked the guard.

'You idiot,' replied the captain, flicking the tip of guard's nose. 'Release the llama. And whoever is sawing at the bars in the window, please stop.'

The scraping noise stopped straight away.

'I can only apologize once again, Miss Gravy,' said the captain, turning to Monica. 'Please be assured that we will do everything we can to find the true culprit.'

'How about checking the CCTV in the shopping mall?' replied Monica smartly.

The captain went quiet for a few seconds. You could almost hear his thoughts rattle across his brain. 'Alonso,' he shouted to the guard, who was unlocking Cruncher's cell. 'Did you check the CCTV footage from the shopping mall?'

'No, Captain, erm . . . I thought you had.'

'IDIOT,' shouted the captain. 'Lock yourself in the cell after you've let the llama out.'

35
THE TOWEL

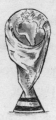

Greg Punch was so confident he was going to be picked for the semi-final with Argentina, he laid out his own kit in the changing room two hours before kick-off. The bright red number eight on his brilliant-white England jersey sparkled under the lights. A shirt he had worn over fifty times – mainly because he had bullied Ray Barnowl into picking him.

Punch's pre-match ritual had been the same for the last ten years. A boiling-hot shower, for at least half an hour, followed by plunging himself into a deep ice bath to make himself really fired up.

He was still in the shower when Tim, McCloud, Ludo, Goal Machine, Motorway and the human members of the England team arrived at the stadium. Molly appeared and swiftly took the llamas and the sheep to 'check the pitch', which is another way of saying 'have a quick wee'. Shhh, don't tell the groundsman.

Tim and McCloud anxiously watched the door on the off chance that Monica would be true to her word and get Cruncher back in time for the match. They were already missing one llama – Lightning was still refusing to let anyone look at her injury.

The sound of Greg Punch singing off tune started to drift from the showers into the changing room.

'Why's he sae bonny?' asked McCloud suspiciously. 'Actually, why is he even here?'

'I guess he thinks that with Cruncher gone, he'll get picked. He is our only other defensive midfielder.'

'Pffftttt,' said McCloud. 'I'd rather play myself than let Greg Punch pull on a pair of boots.'

'You can't play, McCloud,' said Tim.

'Why the Jambos not?' exclaimed McCloud. 'I'm as good as anyone else here, even though I'm a wee bit older.'

'You can't play because you are Scottish,' Tim pointed out.

'Ah . . . yes, of course . . . That thing,' replied McCloud.

Greg Punch emerged from the steam of the showers, with a red-and-white England towel wrapped around himself.

'I'm back, everyone,' he called to the entire room. 'Just when you need me, too. The World Cup semi-final.'

The England team didn't seem overjoyed with Greg Punch's triumphant return. Several of them slumped back into their seats and put their heads in their hands. The positive pre-match energy that should have filled the room before this crucial match was nowhere to be seen.

Punch advanced menacingly on Tim and McCloud, flexing his muscles. Tim tried not to gulp, but couldn't help it. Punch was a big and scary brute, even in a towel. He could see why Ray Barnowl couldn't control him.

'So, I don't see your precious llama, Crunchie,' he said.

'Crunch*er*,' corrected Tim, with a bit of a squeak.

'Whatever,' continued Punch, stepping closer to Tim. 'With him not turning up, and none of these lot able to play in defensive midfield, I think that means you'll have to pick me instead.'

Tim looked up as Punch loomed over him. He'd already had one scuffle with him this tournament; he didn't really want another one. He tried to take another gulp, but his throat was so dry.

'Can't speak, boy?' growled Punch.

'OK, OK, that's quite enough of that, ye sassenach,' said McCloud, barging between Punch and Tim. 'Ye may think you can bully a wee boy, a team of players and a rubbish manager, but ye cannae bully me.'

'Oh, can't I?' replied Punch. He raised his hand and flicked McCloud's cap clean off the top of his head. The cap did a couple of loop-the-loops in the air and landed in a puddle of water from the showers. Several players gasped. Tim was wide-eyed with amazement. He'd never seen the top of McCloud's head before. It was surprisingly hairy.

McCloud looked down at the cap for a few seconds, then bent down to retrieve it. Punch grinned, raised his left foot and with it shoved the Scottish coach on to the floor. The changing room gasped again. Tim was frozen to the spot.

'Cabbage and ribs,' swore McCloud. 'You've gone and doon it now.' He scooped up his cap and fixed it firmly back on his head, then rolled up the sleeves on his tracksuit and got back to his feet. He then took the pose of an old-time heavyweight boxer, legs wide apart, left fist high in the air, the right hand close to his chest.

Punch began to laugh. 'Ha ha ha ha ha,' he cackled.

227

'You going to try and beat me up, old man?'

'Aye,' replied McCloud calmly, eyes focused on his target.

Punch readjusted his towel, then also took a boxer's stance, but it looked far more dangerous than McCloud's. Tim wanted to jump in between them and shout 'STOP', but it felt like someone had nailed his feet to the floor.

The pair began slowly advancing on and circling each other, like a pair of caged tigers. The rest of the England team gathered around Tim and were watching the impending fight, transfixed.

Tim could see Punch's muscles twitch under his skin. He was about to unleash a sledgehammer blow. Punch by name, Punch by nature.

CRAAASSSHHHHHHH, came a deafening noise from the other side of the room. The changing-room door flew off its hinges and smashed on to the floor. There stood Monica, Fiona and a very angry-looking Cruncher.

Cruncher surveyed the room and locked eyes with Punch. The England captain lowered his fists and began backing slowly away, grabbing his towel firmly round his waist. Cruncher started to advance steadily.

'Hey, you!' called Punch to Tim as he staggered around the cluttered changing room trying to keep a safe distance from the menacing Cruncher. 'Call your llama off. CALL HIM OFF.'

Tim shrugged and a wry smile formed in the corner of his mouth. 'He's not a dog, he's a llama, if you hadn't noticed. A professional football-playing llama.'

'CALL HIM OFF,' shouted Punch again. He'd gone very pale.

'His name is Cruncher, and unfortunately our llama expert isn't with us today,' replied Tim, with another shrug.

Punch reached the open door of the changing room, and bolted out into the stadium tunnel.

Cruncher leaped after him, at high speed, chasing him down the tunnel and out on to the pitch.

The 80,000-strong crowd, who were in a joyous pre-match singing mood, suddenly stopped what they were doing and cast their collective gaze to the side of the pitch . . .

To see a man, dressed only in a towel, sprinting as fast as his legs would carry him. And charging behind him was a very angry-looking llama.

'Hey, it's Greg Punch!' shouted a lone voice from

deep among the crowd.

'And Cruncher!' shouted another voice.

The entire 80,000-strong crowd started singing, 'CRUNCHER . . . CRUNCHER . . . CRUNCHER . . . CRUNCHER,' as the llama started gaining ground on the tiring England midfielder.

Disaster struck. Well, disaster for Greg Punch, but nobody wants him to win, do they? He tripped on the edge of his towel and was sent sprawling across the pitch.

Cruncher stood over him and snorted loudly.

'EAT HIM . . . EAT HIM . . . EAT HIM . . . EAT HIM . . . EAT HIM,' came the chant from the crowd.

Cruncher looked round the stadium then lowered his large tooth-filled mouth towards Greg Punch.

'EEEEEEEEEEEEEEEEEEEEEE,' squeaked Punch, closing his eyes and putting his hands over his face. He had no idea that llamas don't eat humans.

Cruncher grabbed the corner of Punch's towel and began gobbling it up. The crowd began howling with laughter at the naked man stranded in the middle of the pitch.

'THERE HE IS!' came a shout from a megaphone. It was Captain Kneeslide. 'ARREST THAT MAN.'

An entire squad of Mucho Plata police officers flooded on to the turf. Greg Punch leaped to his feet and scampered across the pitch, protecting himself with his hands. He didn't get very far and was quickly rugby tackled by a member of Captain Kneeslide's team.

The crowd cheered its approval as Punch was escorted away. We won't be hearing from him for a long time.

Cruncher stood in the middle of the pitch, ignoring the fracas that was going on around him. He was still casually chewing on the tasty England towel. This was definitely one of the best ones yet. Then again, he always thought that.

36
WORLD CUP SEMI-FINAL: ENGLAND V ARGENTINA

Argentina were a strange team: a mixture of gritty hard men and skilful, talented players. Their captain was a fiery little man called Pablo Trueno, which, if my basic Spanish is working, roughly translates as 'Paul Thunder', and he was rated as one of the best players in the world.

All great players – apart from me, of course – usually have one single weakness. Maybe it's heading or tackling, or perhaps they're not as fast as they'd like. For Trueno, it wasn't something he could avoid. He had a terrible temper. He would regularly explode at his own teammates, other teams, TV reporters and the man serving coffee in the local shop – though he always forgot to put the sugar in his latte, so maybe it was understandable.

When he wasn't shouting at everyone, Trueno was an exceptional football player. It was like someone had tied the ball to his foot with a piece of string. He was already top scorer at this World Cup with five goals, and was looking for more.

Now the Punch situation was over, Tim had a few minutes to think about his tactics before kick-off. His squad was bolstered by Punch's Nork Town cronies, who suddenly offered their apologies and asked if they could rejoin the team now they were free from Punch's clutches. But Tim didn't really need them. He knew that to stop Argentina, you had to stop Trueno, and Cruncher was just the llama for the job, even though he had just spent the night in jail and eaten a whole towel.

Tim found a picture of Trueno and showed it to Cruncher over and over and over again, while the rest of the team warmed up. Cruncher just stood there looking at the picture. He didn't seem to be that bothered by it. Tim ran round the dressing room with the picture of Trueno making sure Cruncher was watching his every move.

The bell in the changing room rang and the England team began leaving for the game. Cruncher just stood there, looking at Tim.

'Go on, Cruncher, off you go. It's the big game. You are marking their best player,' he said, urging the llama to follow his teammates out of the room.

Cruncher continued to stand and look at him.

'C'mon, Cruncher, let's do this,' pleaded Tim, approaching the llama and patting him on the back. 'I know you've had a difficult day, but our World Cup dream is counting on you!'

Cruncher leaned down and grabbed the picture of Trueno out of Tim's hand and began eating it. The picture was gone in less than ten seconds. Tim knew Cruncher was ready. But was Trueno ready for Cruncher?

The crowd was in fine voice as the referee blew his whistle to start the match. Trueno immediately received the ball and began a run through the heart of the England midfield. He got as far as the edge of the area, and was about to pull the trigger when Cruncher arrived, sliding through to expertly take the ball. Trueno crashed into the turf and began rolling around as if he'd been shot. Although I'm sure if you were shot, you wouldn't roll over and over nine times. The referee waved 'play on'.

Trueno eventually got to his feet, after banging the pitch with his fist a few times, and began moaning to anyone that would listen. Moments later, he was back on the ball, his tantrum forgotten. This time he dodged several tackles and found himself clear, charging down the left-hand side of the pitch. All he'd have to do was whip in a cross to one of his unmarked teammates in the area and . . . *Kkkeeeerrrrspplllaaattt.* Trueno found his face planted into the pitch once again. It was Cruncher with another brilliantly executed tackle.

If you marked Trueno's anger levels on a scale of one to ten, he was already at fifteen. Although he had started the match on a nine, after discovering someone had eaten one of his pre-match chocolate mousses.

The game continued like this for the rest of the half. Trueno was having brilliant game until he got to Cruncher, who was having an even better match. There was just no way past him. Half-time score:

ENGLAND 0 – 0 ARGENTINA

At the start of the second half, England were flying, but they couldn't break down the Argentinians. Goal Machine hit the crossbar twice, Steakhouse had a one-on-one expertly stopped, and Melonhead saw his towering header cleared off the goal line.

Meanwhile Trueno was reaching boiling point. Everywhere he turned there was Cruncher blocking his way, a llama-shaped shadow.

In the sixty-ninth minute Trueno finally exploded. Cruncher expertly tackled him inside his own area and nutmegged the Argentinian player twice, before casually passing the ball downfield. Trueno leaped up, believing once again he had been terribly fouled, and began squaring up to Cruncher, pressing his forehead on to the llama's head. Cruncher responded to this by eating a bit of the Argentinian's curly hair.

A load of players from both sides stepped in and began pushing and shoving each other around the England penalty area. Then the referee joined in and tried to calm everything down, but this just made it worse. He reached for his pocket to show a yellow card to Trueno, and then all hell broke loose.

Trueno began angrily waving his arms around, and then he did the worst thing you could ever do to a referee (apart from stealing his half-time biscuits). He placed both his hands on the ref's shoulders, and gave him a gentle shove. The crowd gasped as one. They couldn't believe what they were seeing. The ref staggered back a few paces, and then his legs buckled from under him, and he crashed down on to the pitch in a heap. It was as if he had been charged by a rhino (though it was actually just a little push). He rolled around on the floor nine times and began holding his knee in pain. A physio ran on to help him up, even though there wasn't actually anything wrong with him.

Trueno knew he was in big trouble, and didn't need to see he was about to be shown the red card. Under a hail of words too rude for this book, he left the pitch and stormed off down the tunnel, never to be seen again. Well, not until he had served a fifteen-game ban.

Argentina were down to ten men and, back in the changing room, their best player was crying into a hot bath. Now was the time for a bold tactical move – Tim had to throw everyone forward for the win.

Argentina struggled without Trueno and were under heavy pressure for the last fifteen minutes of the game. Goal Machine, Cruncher, Tablecloth,

Melonhead and Useless all had good chances to give England the lead, but were thwarted by the excellent Argentinian keeper and some very brave last-ditch blocks by the defenders in front of him.

Just as Tim was beginning to think about extra time and the possibility of penalties to decide the match, T. J. Wilkinson broke clear of the Argentinian left back and floated a high cross into the area. It was perhaps too high. The tall Argentinian keeper left his six-yard box and began to jump towards the ball to punch it away, but he was joined by an England player also jumping to challenge for the ball. It was the huge defender Sid Melonhead, and like the keeper he also appeared to have his hand slightly above his head.

What happened next was a bit of blur. The two players collided and the ball flew back up into the air and then spun back towards the Argentinian net. The Argentina defenders charged back to clear the ball, but they were too late. The ball bounced once and then hopped over the line.

ENGLAND 1 – 0 ARGENTINA!!

Melonhead picked himself off the ground and ran away to celebrate. The Argentinian team went mad, running up to the ref pointing at their hands. They clearly felt that Melonhead had punched the ball into the net. The ref was having none of it, firmly pointing back to the centre circle to get the game restarted.

Tim was trying to remain as calm as possible on the outside, but on the inside it felt like someone had lit a firework. If it stayed like this, England would be in the World Cup final for the first time in years. He watched the last few minutes with his hands over his eyes. Every time the Argentinians got the ball, it felt like his heart was about to burst through his chest. Every time an England player had the ball, he would experience a wave of relief. The last five minutes felt like they were lasting an hour. Had the clock stopped or something?

McCloud was going mad in the technical area. 'GET IT IN THE CORNER, RUN IT IN THE CORNER, IN THE CORNER,' he would shout every time an England player got the ball. The llamas totally ignored this instruction and seemed determined to score another goal. Which made McCloud even madder. 'IN . . . THE . . . CORNER,' he screamed until his whole head had gone totally purple.

It was the goal-scoring hero Melonhead who had the final touch. He smashed the ball high into the stands, and the ref finally blew his whistle.

FULL-TIME: ENGLAND 1 – 0 ARGENTINA!

Tim couldn't believe it. He charged on to the pitch with McCloud, the rest of the subs and backroom staff, and celebrated with the players and the llamas. Well, the llamas didn't really celebrate, they just munched on the pitch. England were in the final of the World Cup! It was the most amazing feeling. But there was one thing Tim was missing – Cairo.

37
GERMAN TRAINING

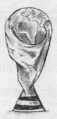

You won't be surprised to hear that Germany had cruised through their matches and would face England in the final. We'd have a bit of a problem if they hadn't reached the final, wouldn't we? I'd have to start the story all over again.

Germany's progress had been very smooth. They had beaten Colombia in the second round, Mexico in the quarter-finals, and France in the semi-final. They still hadn't let in a goal and it had all been so easy, their manager Geoff Coren had hardly left his seat in the dugout. This team didn't need any encouragement, they basically managed themselves, especially with someone like Karl-Heinz Torstooper in goal.

Cairo watched all of Germany's matches from the posh seats where the families sat, and clapped and cheered at the right moments. But deep in his heart he missed being down on the pitch with Tim and

McCloud, keeping an eye on the llamas. Football was even more boring when you weren't involved.

Geoff Coren was now popping into Torstooper's hotel suite at all hours of the day, worrying about what was going to happen in the final with England.

'I can't lose to a team of llamas again, it will ruin my reputation,' he told Torstooper and Prussia, as he twiddled nervously with his lovely enormous hair.

'You have already told Torstooper this,' said Torstooper bluntly. 'Torstooper told you not to worry. Germany will win the World Cup. The Golden Octopus will be too good for the llamas.'

'He still hasn't let in a goal all tournament,' added Prussia proudly.

'I just can't have them win again,' continued Coren, ignoring the two Germans. 'I just can't. I just can't.' His eyes were wide and bloodshot; he'd clearly been up all night worrying since the two finalists had qualified.

'This man is still an idiot,' added Prussia in German. 'Why he was given the Germany job I will never know. He has done nothing to help our cause. You have done it all. You should be made Germany manager, not this gibbering Englishman.'

Torstooper nodded at his agent and started his

translation to Coren: 'He says you are a fantastic manager and you shouldn't worry about England. Germany are too strong for them. We will win.'

Coren laughed, an uneasy, manic laugh that went on too long. 'I do hope he is right. You'll never know what it feels like to be embarrassed by a team of llamas. I can't go through that again. I just can't.'

The day before the final, Cairo arrived at the German camp to discover Torstooper had been summoned for some medical tests and wouldn't be back until later that day. He had left Prussia in sole charge of Cairo.

Cairo didn't really want to spend the day with just Prussia – all he really talked about was other footballers, and how much he disliked them. However, the other option was going back to the England camp and possibly dealing with Tim, and he didn't fancy that either. Another day in front of the TV drinking milkshakes with Prussia was slightly better.

Cairo would have been the first to admit the TV, milkshake and games-console routine in the German camp was becoming a little boring, and he was really missing spending time with the llamas. But he knew it was just until the World Cup was over, and then he could go home with his mum and get away from the non-stop football. In the holidays he could spend time with his dad in Germany, where apparently you could eat sausages for every meal . . . even breakfast.

With Torstooper away, Prussia became a lot more active. He appeared with a whistle around his neck and a clipboard in his hands.

'You are coming with me now,' he boomed at Cairo. 'I am fed up with sitting around all day doing nothing. Your training will start today. We have already wasted enough time.'

'Training?' replied Cairo apprehensively.

'Yes, training. The son of the great Torstooper must begin training.'

'But Dad never said anything about training.'

'That is because he is focused on winning the World Cup,' said Prussia, handing Cairo a bright yellow bib. 'You don't want to disappoint your father, now do you? He has given you everything you desire, it is now time to train.'

'But I thought I was just spending time with Dad here, until the World Cup ended.'

'Pppfffttt, all this sitting around is not good for you,' replied Prussia. 'You are becoming fat. Training is the most important.'

Cairo didn't like the sound of this. Something was

up. But he didn't want to annoy his dad, especially as he was only just starting to get to know him. Perhaps he should see what Prussia wanted.

Worst. Mistake. Ever! Prussia put Cairo through a training routine so intense, he was sick four times. Three of them out of his nose. He ran laps of the pitch, sprinted from one penalty area to another, hopped across tiny ankle-height metal fences, did press-ups, sit-ups, squat thrusts and star jumps. All while Prussia shouted at him in a mixture of English and German. Cairo had no idea what was going on – it wasn't good.

When Prussia finally stopped training it was already past lunchtime, and Cairo was so tired he could have fallen asleep on the side of the pitch. Prussia didn't look at all happy. He had already snapped his walking stick in half when watching Cairo attempt press-ups and punched through his straw hat when he failed his first sit-up.

After a feeble lunch of water and the crust off a loaf of bread, Prussia had Cairo training again, even harder than he had during the morning session. Cairo didn't get the impression Prussia thought he was getting any better.

As Cairo was slowly jogging his eighteenth lap of the afternoon, he could see a tall figure approaching in the distance. His heart skipped a beat: it was his dad returning from his medical tests. Surely he would see what Prussia was doing and stop the training immediately.

Prussia intercepted Torstooper and started furiously talking to him. Waving and swishing his spare walking stick about like he was in some medieval battle. Torstooper calmly stood by him and listened. Cairo had hoped his dad would calm his angry agent down, but he seemed to be nodding along to what he said. Surely that couldn't be right?

Eventually the two Germans came over to Cairo and told him to stop. Cairo crashed to his knees and began gulping in air. He had never felt so exhausted. He certainly wasn't any type of athlete, and if he was honest with himself, he had no desire to be one either. Best he stuck with caring for animals.

'Torstooper has been told that Torstooper's son is struggling with his training,' said Torstooper coldly, as though he was talking to a fridge rather than his son.

'What's he . . . what's he . . . doing to me, Dad?' asked Cairo, when he had finally got his breath back. 'I think . . . I think . . . I should go back to the llamas. Lightning is . . . injured after all. This training isn't for me.'

'He is training you to become the next greatest goalkeeper in the world. Keeping the famous Torstooper goalkeeping name alive after Torstooper retires. You will become the perfect replacement for Torstooper. From your performance today it sounds like we should have started you earlier.'

Cairo pulled a face. 'I'm not a footballer,' he said with a sneer. 'I can hardly kick a ball in a straight line.'

'You have the blood of Torstooper in your veins,' said Prussia. 'You will become great, with intense training every day until your sixteenth birthday.'

'Not sure I like the sound of that,' said Cairo.

'I will be your agent throughout this process,

making sure you make the right commercial decisions,' added Prussia.

'Commercial decisions?' questioned Cairo.

'Where all your money comes from,' explained Prussia. 'I will make you rich. Richer than you could ever imagine.'

'Well, it sounds like you've done a fantastic job of sorting this all out, but it's not really me, I'm afraid,' said Cairo as politely as he could. 'I'm more of a stopping-hedgehogs-getting-run-over kind of person, rather than a stopping-balls-going-in-a-net kind of person.'

Prussia waved his stick at Cairo. 'You will watch Torstooper win the World Cup tomorrow and then you will join me at my intense training camp in the Schwarzwald. Here you will stay.'

'This is how Torstooper became great,' said Torstooper robotically.

'But you missed being part of a family, and missed the birth of your son,' said Cairo bitterly.

Torstooper took a slight step backwards, as though Cairo's last sentence had chipped a chunk off his cold stone heart.

'Torstooper wasn't aware of this family,' he said eventually, in a hushed tone.

Prussia looked impatient. 'We don't have time for this family business. It was a long time ago and a lot of time has passed. You are together now. It's a perfect time for you to start your training and become a legend. I have already booked our flights to the Schwarzwald.'

'Er, I'm not sure you can do that,' said Cairo. He was getting really upset that his dad didn't seem to want to stop this silly plan. 'You can't force me to go anywhere.'

'Ah but we can – you signed a contract,' said Prussia, waving a piece of paper in Cairo's face.

'No, I didn't,' said Cairo frantically. 'I didn't sign anything.'

'Your signature is here,' said Prussia pointing at what looked like Cairo's signature scrawl on the bottom of a long official document.

'The only thing I've signed for is room-service milkshake,' said Cairo.

'Sometimes milkshakes and official football contracts get mixed up, don't they?' said Prussia with a cruel laugh.

'You cheat!' shouted Cairo as Prussia escorted him back to the hotel. 'You can't do this, you've trapped me. Dad, help me! DAD, PLEASE!'

Torstooper stood still. He clearly wasn't sure what he should do next. Football was his life, all he had thought about over the last twenty years. Emotional and business decisions had always been down to Prussia. Finding out he had a son was incredibly confusing. He moved slowly towards Cairo as if to comfort him, but was quickly stopped.

'What are you doing?' shouted Prussia at Torstooper, as he dragged Cairo back into the hotel. 'You have a World Cup final to train for. Your final match. Get on with it.'

38
NIGHT-TIME WORRIES

Cairo sat in an armchair in a room back at the German camp. His stay certainly wasn't quite so much fun now. Prussia had contacted Molly and spun her a story that they were all going to a 'fantastic dinner with the royal family' and it was best if Cairo continued to stay with them for another evening.

Cairo felt terrible, and totally alone. He had ditched his best friend to be with a dad who didn't seem to really care about him. He had ignored the llamas, and he had left his mum behind to look after them all. He'd even neglected Lightning while she was carrying an injury. What a fool he had been. He had been tricked by his dad's agent and a few delicious milkshakes. Now he was totally trapped.

The World Cup final was tomorrow and he was stuck in the German HQ. There was no escape. Prussia made sure he couldn't communicate with the outside world. All he had in his room was a bed, a lamp and a lot of scatter cushions. Cairo felt so gloomy, all he could do was lie on his bed and try and get to sleep. His legs and arms were throbbing from all the training and needed the rest, but he couldn't turn his brain off.

On the other side of Cairo's door was Geoff Coren, pacing around the three huge sofas in the penthouse lounge. He looked like he had been scared by a thousand ghosts in just one hour. He was as white as sheet and his hair was firing off in huge crazy directions. He was nervously rubbing his hands together and chewing frantically on his bottom lip.

'What is the problem *now*, Geoff Coren?' asked Torstooper.

'The man has gone mad,' said Prussia, in German. 'This idiot is a gibbering wreck.'

'I can't let the llamas beat us in the World Cup tomorrow,' said Coren rapidly, not understanding Prussia. He began rubbing the bags under his eyes. He had hardly slept in the last four days, because he had been worrying about the llamas. When he did occasionally drop off, his dreams would be full of Ludo, Lightning, Cruncher and Goal Machine prancing around a supermarket, working on the deli counter, in the bakery, stacking shelves and beeping the items through the tills. Geoff Coren always dreamed about supermarkets. He was born in the yogurt aisle of his parents' local store.

'How many times have we been through this?' said Torstooper. He was getting really bored of Coren and his llama obsession.

'If England win tomorrow, that's it, my career is over. The most talented manager in the history of the game, lost.'

Then an evil grin spread itself across his face

'But they won't win,' Coren said fiercely. 'I've come up with a plan to make sure that we are guaranteed victory.'

Prussia and Torstooper looked quizzically at the huge-haired manager.

'I'm going to make sure that the England team find it incredibly hard to play the match.' An evil glint flashed across his eyes.

'How is this?' asked Torstooper warily.

'Oh, I can't tell you, that's my secret. My delicious Italian secret,' said Coren, adding a wild cackle and tapping the side of his nose. 'HHAAAAAA HHHAAAAA. You will know when the time comes, mark my words. Those llamas won't trouble me again after this, and I'll have a lovely golden trophy on my shelf and the pick of the best clubs in the world to manage.'

Coren did a very unusual star-jump celebration in the middle of the room and then quickly left.

'This man is still an idiot,' said Prussia in German to Torstooper. 'A very crazy idiot.'

Torstooper ignored his agent. He was deep in thought. Whatever this plan was, it didn't sound right.

On the other side of the island, Tim lay in bed, his eyes wide open and his feet all slippery with sweat. It felt like it was Christmas Eve and he was waiting for Santa to arrive. He looked at the orange digital clock by his bed. The bright green display showed 3.34 a.m. Urggghh, tonight was taking ages, he thought. It was definitely 3.32 a.m. about an hour ago.

As everyone knows, 3.34 a.m. is the best time to do some really silly worrying. Did I write my homework in black or blue biro? Which is better, curly or crinkle-cut chips? Did I actually save that computer game before I turned the console off? What will happen if I put on my sister's pants for school by mistake? All the really important stuff.

Tim worried about the team, and whether his tactics were going to be good enough to beat Germany, or even good enough to get a shot past the seemingly unbeatable Torstooper. That made him think about his so-called friend Cairo. Perhaps he had been a bit selfish, putting the England team over Cairo's long-lost dad. Tim couldn't imagine what it would be like not to have a dad when you're growing up. His had always been around. Even when he was really annoying and uncool, Frank was still around to help him out and do all the things dads do. Like paying for computer games, new boots and balls, driving him to places or collecting takeaway pizza. Cairo only had his mum for all that. It must have been tough for her as a single parent, too.

Tim cursed himself. He'd blown it now though. Cairo was with the German team and might never come back. Tomorrow would be the biggest day of his life and he wasn't going to share it with his best mate.

He rolled over and looked at the clock again.

3.35 a.m.

39
THE ESCAPE

TAP, TAP, TAP, TAP, came a faint noise from the en-suite bathroom. TAP, TAP, TAP, TAP, it sounded again.

Cairo sat up and rubbed his eyes. He must have finally fallen asleep for a few minutes.

TAP, TAP, TAP, TAP.

Cairo clambered out of bed and staggered to the bathroom, stubbing his toe on the corner of the bed, which is easily the worst pain ever invented. After ten minutes hopping around the room, he entered the bathroom.

TAP, TAP, TAP, TAP.

Cairo looked at the tap, then put his ear to it.

TAP, TAP, TAP, TAP.

Not that, he thought, even though this is the noise taps usually make. They are very big-headed and love shouting out their own names.

The noise wasn't coming from the bath or the lovely powerful shower. It was coming from the large vent in the ceiling.

TAP, TAP, TAP, TAP. Louder now. Cairo had lifted his head towards the vent.

'Hello?' he whispered into it, which felt a little odd.

A thin periscope shot down through a gap in the vent, and bashed Cairo on the top of his head.

'OWWWW,' said Cairo pulling a scrunchy face, and rubbing his head.

'When I give the signal, pull the vent away from the ceiling,' hissed a nasal voice from behind the periscope.

The screws attaching the vent to the ceiling began unwinding themselves, the sound of an electric tool speedily doing the job.

'Pull the vent away,' came the nasal voice again as the periscope disappeared back up into the ceiling.

Cairo stuck his fingers into the vent and gave it a huge tug. It dislodged and he was showered with dust and other mucky bits and pieces that had probably been up there for years.

Two faces peered down from the hole in the ceiling. One was a ninja and the other was a frogman.

'Fiona?' asked Cairo uncertainly. 'Er, Frank?'

The duo both put their thumbs up and removed their masks. Frank looked thoroughly fed up.

Being a henchman in Fiona's 'ninja squad', as she called it, was incredibly annoying. He loved his daughter dearly and would do anything for her, but driving her everywhere, helping her to break into places and saving people from hotel bathrooms wasn't something he had expected to do. What made it even worse was that she wanted all the glory – he was supposed to be invisible. He wasn't even allowed to wear a ninja costume.

'You weren't at the "fantastic dinner with the royal family", so I knew you were being kept here as a prisoner,' said Fiona dramatically. 'Now's the time to escape.'

Cairo didn't need to think twice. The prospect of becoming some kind of super-goalkeeper who never stopped training didn't really fill him with any pleasure. Even if it meant being with his dad. He missed the llamas, Tim and even McCloud. They were much more fun.

'Put this on,' said Fiona, throwing him down a bright pink plastic Mexican wrestler's mask. 'It's all I had left in my mask store.'

'Do I need a mask?'

'Of course,' replied Fiona, 'You are in my ninja squad now, we have to travel in secret. Your secret ninja number is now number two.'

'Hey, why aren't I number two?' moaned Frank. 'I've been in the ninja squad longer.'

'Quiet, number seventeen,' snapped Fiona. 'We don't have time for this, we have to get back quickly. The things I do for my brother!'

40
WORLD CUP FINAL DAY

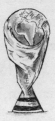

Tim, McCloud, the llamas and the rest of the England team had gone to the Big Sparkly Diamond Stadium super-early to get the feel of the place before the World Cup final kick-off. It certainly lived up to expectations.

It was a huge 150,000-seater stadium, with four enormous marble towers standing guard around it, a wonder of modern architecture swaddled in glass and metal. Even McCloud hadn't seen anything like it, and according to him he'd played at every big ground in the entire world. He stood there gazing up into the sky, opening and shutting his mouth, totally speechless. This must have been a first, thought Tim.

Standing outside the gates was a very familiar figure. It was Cairo, and he looked like he'd been stuck in an air vent for three hours.

Tim felt his heart do a little somersault as he saw

his friend, but he was going to be cautious. His mind was racing. Cairo could be here to steal his tactics ahead of the biggest game ever. There was no other reason for him to be here. He had shown zero interest in the progress of England so far.

Cairo approached Tim very slowly and awkwardly. He kept looking down at his feet.

'Hi,' he said sheepishly.

'Er, hi,' replied Tim just as sheepishly.

'You all right?' said Cairo.

'I suppose,' replied Tim, with a shrug. He really wanted to tell Cairo he was incredibly nervous about the game.

There was a long, awkward pause between the two. You could hear the cars and mopeds tooting and peeping on the roads around the ground.

'Soooo,' said Cairo slowly. 'I think I sort of made a mistake.'

'Oh?' said Tim hopefully.

'My dad wasn't the person I expected him to be,' continued Cairo. 'Plus, I miss the llamas, and being with the team.' He paused again before he said another sentence and uneasily looked at his shoes. 'I also sort of miss hanging out with you.'

'Oh,' said Tim. 'Erm, I sort of missed hanging

out with you, too.' Tim also looked at the floor. 'I'm sorry for being so angry about football all the time.'

McCloud, who had been eavesdropping the conversation while pretending to tie his bootlaces, even though he was wearing flip-flops, stepped in, shaking his head.

'Urgghh, laddies, this is painful,' he groaned. 'Look, we all know Cairo's sorry for leaving the team and Tim is sorry for caring more about the team than Cairo's dad. Plus, we also worked out that Cairo's dad is a bit of a rotten haggis. I could have told you that before all this started, but naebody asked me. So basically everyone wants Cairo back in the team. I know the llamas would get a real wee boost from it.'

The two boys nodded.

'OK, that's settled then,' added McCloud. 'Shake hands, and let's get on with winning this Cup final.'

Tim and Cairo shook hands, and then gave each other a big hug.

Molly appeared leading the llamas and Motorway towards the stadium. Her eyes lit up when she saw her son.

'Oh, Cairo, you're here?' she said. 'You came back to be with the England team?'

'Yes, I'm sorry I walked out on you guys for Dad.

He wasn't who I expected him to be. I should have spent more time with you.'

'He wasn't always like that, Cairo. There's still some of the old Dad in there somewhere, I'm sure of it.'

'He didn't know you were having a baby,' continued Cairo.

'Didn't he?' replied Molly quizzically. 'I told his agent, that Prussia chap, to pass on a message, not long before they left.'

'He didn't tell him,' said Cairo miserably.

Molly wiped her eyes on the side of her sleeve and took a deep breath. 'Well, we can't do anything about that now, can we? I'm sure we can work it out with your dad. The important thing is you're back where you belong. With us.'

Lightning limped across to Cairo and began nuzzling his face. Cairo chuckled, then remembered.

'Oh, Lightning, I'm so sorry! I totally forgot about your injury. Let me have a look at it.'

He knelt down and carefully lifted the llama's damaged foot. Tim, McCloud and Molly all marvelled at how easy he made it look. With his fingers acting as a pincer, Cairo began digging around in between Lightning's toes. The llama didn't flinch a bit, she just bravely let Cairo get to work. A few seconds later Cairo was proudly brandishing a sharp thorn that had been lodged in Lightning's foot. It wasn't ligament damage, a strain or a bruise after all.

'Simple,' said Cairo. 'I can't see what all the fuss was about.'

41
THE SUSPICIOUS LASAGNE

The Big Sparkly Diamond Stadium was even more impressive on the inside. Five tiers of red and black seating surrounded a huge, lush green pitch. The goalposts and pitch markings sparkled in the afternoon sun, as flags of every single country that had played in the tournament fluttered in the light breeze.

On the pitch, a team of groundsmen and pitch consultants were making sure that every blade of grass was absolutely perfect ahead of the biggest match of the year. Nothing would be left to chance.

Noisy clumps of fans were starting to trickle into the stadium as an electric atmosphere was building. Frank, Beetroot, Monica and Fiona took their seats, all their faces painted with the England flag. In the corner of the ground, Molly led the 'holiday llamas' into a special pen by the side of the pitch so they could watch the match too. They were on their best behaviour for the first time all tournament. Shaved into their hairy coats were the letters E, N, G, L, A and N. Smasher refused to have the D shaved into his . . . I've told you, he didn't like to make a fuss.

If McCloud had been quiet outside, he was totally silent inside. Tim looked at his old Scottish coach and was positive he could see a little tear in the corner of his eye.

'I think McCloud is crying,' he whispered to Cairo.

'Has someone stolen his tracksuit and cap?' joked Cairo, and the pair shared a little chuckle for the first time in ages.

The players and llamas were out on the pitch going through their warm-up routines. Well, the players were. The llamas just stood about nibbling at the grass.

'It's great to see the llamas again,' said Cairo. 'I realize now I was missing them loads. Watching the German team was like looking at a high-performing engine, and engines are really boring. England are much more fun.'

'They certainly are now,' said Tim. Having Cairo back made him forget that his stomach had been doing cartwheels ever since they arrived at the ground. He looked at his fingernails, which he had already bitten down as far as they could go. Then the worry gushed back into his stomach.

'I think I'm going to go to the toilet again,' said Tim, and he sprinted off.

The players finished their warm-up, trooped back into the changing room and began preparing for the match, which was in less than an hour's time. Gold tiles decorated the walls, and each player had a smart individual changing area with a comfy seat and a little cupboard to store all their stuff. There was even a special fenced-off area for the llamas and Motorway to relax in, packed with grass, fresh straw and other tasty goodies. In the middle of the room was a huge table piled high with fruit, energy drinks, chocolate bars, jellies, ice cream, sweeties and, of course, chocolate mousse. It looked amazing. The people of Mucho Plata were treating them like royalty.

There was knock on the door and a very smart waiter wheeled a huge silver trolley into the changing room. Perched on top of the trolley was a huge lasagne. The best-looking, best-smelling crispy-edged lasagne you could ever imagine. Planted in the middle of the lasagne was a tall metal skewer with a note attached.

> Dear England team,
>   Congratulations on reaching the final of the World Cup. This is an amazing achievement considering just three weeks ago you were really rubbish. You should be very proud of yourselves.
>   The whole country is totally behind you and we have our fingers and toes crossed that you will be able to bring the famous trophy back to England this time. It has been away for far too long.
>   Love, hugs and big kisses,
>   Princess Candice

For those of you who don't know, Princess Candice was the stunningly beautiful member of the Mucho Plata royal family. She was also half English, and a fantastic carpenter, although that's not important here..

'It's from Princess Candice,' said Sid Melonhead excitedly. He had always really liked her.

'Wow, Princess Candice – she's my favourite,' added Chaz Steakhouse.

The rest of the team crowded round the lasagne and made 'coo' and 'wow' noises at it.

The lasagne was certainly the most charming and bewitching layers of tomato, meat, cheese and sheets of pasta ever to be cooked. Coming from someone as lovely as Princess Candice, it was even better. She was easily the best royal person ever to wear a crown.

'I'm nae sure we should be eating lasagne this close to an important game,' said McCloud from the other side of the room.

'Ah, one small mouthful won't hurt us,' replied Tim, also captivated by the delicious-looking lasagne. 'It's from the royal family after all.'

'Pasta is great for energy levels, and anyway you told me once you used to eat steak and chips before you played a football match,' added Cairo, grabbing a huge metal serving slice and plunging it deep into the melted cheesy layers.

The players crowded around Cairo, holding plates

that they'd somehow got their hands on, all licking their lips as the incredible lasagne smell wafted into their nostrils.

'Hurry up with the serving,' one of them shouted as Cairo began to carefully divide up portions for the entire playing squad and all the backroom team. He was trying to make it fair just in case someone moaned, which footballers tend to do.

Then there was another knock on the door. A loud, thunderous hammering, probably done with a clenched fist rather than the knuckles. T. J. Wilkinson opened the door and there, towering in the doorframe, was Karl-Heinz Torstooper dressed in his German tracksuit. He didn't look happy. Was he looking for the escaped Cairo?

Cairo dropped the serving slice and tried to melt into the throng of players. He didn't want his dad to find him, especially not in his biggest rivals' changing room.

Torstooper began advancing robotically into the room. Sid Melonhead tried to block his way but was brushed aside. Torstooper started unravelling a large piece of foil. Cairo began cowering behind some of the players. He didn't want to be wrapped up in foil and taken back to the German team.

'Hey, what are you doing?' shouted Tim, jumping in front of the huge German keeper.

Torstooper ignored him and continued his mechanical march. Tim, like Melonhead, was brushed aside. The other England players started getting involved and began trying to block and pull back the German, but he was too strong for them all. Soon he was nearly on top of Cairo as he tried to crunch himself into a protective ball on the floor beside the table. Cairo held his hands above his head to protect himself from the foil and closed his eyes . . .

Nothing happened, except the sound of foil being wrapped over something else. Wrapped over something cheesy, meaty, tomato-y and pasta-y, something that seconds ago had put the rest of the room in a trance.

'Hey, that's our shepherd's pie,' shouted Steve Crispy.

'It's a lasagne, you idiot,' remarked Sid Melonhead.

'Hey, that's our laz-ag-knecer!' said Steve Crispy.

Torstooper lifted the lasagne off the table and began carrying it away.

'This is not your lasagne, and it is not from your lovely Princess Candice. It is a trick. It has been poisoned by somebody who should know better,' said

Torstooper, without a flicker of emotion. 'Torstooper does not want to win the World Cup by cheating. Torstooper wants to win the World Cup on proper terms. Two teams playing the best they can. Good luck to you all.'

He turned to look at Cairo, gave him a friendly wink, and then left the changing room.

'Now that, lads, is a proper fitballer. One of the greatest in the world,' said McCloud. 'Now let's go out there and beat his team. Fair and square.'

42
WORLD CUP FINAL: ENGLAND V GERMANY (FIRST HALF)

Geoff Coren looked surprised to see the whole England team lining up for the match. He was expecting a few of them to be stuck in the toilet, having consumed his poisonous lasagne. Not deadly poison of course, he's not that evil. Perhaps the poison hadn't kicked in yet, he thought. He would have to keep an eye out for the England players suddenly having to dash off the pitch and not come back.

A few important men in suits shuffled out to greet the players before kick-off. Then the crowd and players both heartily sang their countries' national anthems. Well, the llamas didn't. They don't know the words. Tim felt as though he was in the middle of a dream. The crowd in the ground, millions around the world on TV, and even Greg Punch in his prison cell were watching. Everyone was ready for kick-off.

'Tim . . . TIM!!!' shouted Cairo. 'Wakey-wakey.'

He snapped his fingers a few times in front of his friend's face. Tim returned to planet Earth and blinked a few times at the pitch.

'It's started, Tim. Stop staring into space like a zombie.'

The game had started, and Germany were already on the attack. One of their midfielders tried his luck from thirty yards, but it was easily dealt with by Ludo, who casually tapped the ball away with his left foot.

Tim looked to the other end of the pitch, and there was Torstooper, patrolling his area and barking orders out to his team. If they were going to win this, they had to find a way past the magnificent German keeper. That amazing save he made in their first match back in the group stages was still playing over and over in his mind.

The game ebbed and flowed throughout the first half with nobody able to make an impact. Finals are always like this. Nobody wants to make a mistake so they are all ultra-careful. Goal Machine was being closely marked by a large German defender, while Lightning was struggling to go on any of her famous runs down the wing. Cruncher was having a good game, breaking up play and passing the ball to his skilful teammates. Ludo was doing his job comfortably, and Motorway hadn't been hit by the ball yet. The match was . . . boring.

HALF-TIME: ENGLAND 0 – 0 GERMANY

It was a massive improvement for England on the last time the two teams met.

'This is a massive improvement on the last time we met,' said McCloud in the changing rooms during the break. 'Dinnae be too downhcarted. We are still in an excellent position.'

'We just need to get some shots on the German goal,' added Tim. 'You can't be afraid of Torstooper. He's just a man, like you lot.'

'Er . . . not the llamas,' added Cairo, with a cough.

Tim chuckled. Then Cairo addressed the room, which he didn't usually tend to do – that was McCloud and Tim's job.

'Look, Tim is right. Torstooper might seem like this unbeatable wall, but he's just a man. He's my dad, and he has weaknesses like everyone else here.'

The England team leaned in to hear about Torstooper's weaknesses.

'OK, maybe his weaknesses aren't football–related.'

A sigh of disappointment washed over the room.

'But . . . he forgets to put the toilet seat down, he leaves crumbs in the butter, he doesn't like sprouts and he doesn't care about llamas.'

'Is there any point to this?' called Sid Melonhead from the back of the room.

'All I'm saying is, don't be afraid of him.' Cairo sat down, slightly disappointed that his little speech didn't seem to have worked.

A murmur of chat went round the room.

'He's right, you know,' bellowed T. J. Wilkinson, standing on his chair. 'We've got to test him, we've go to show no fear, or we might as well just stay here for the second half. LET'S DO THIS.'

The England team jumped up and began stamping their feet on the ground, and banging the walls with their fists. Even the four llamas and Motorway started making some unusual baa-ing bleating noises. The almighty racket made energy surge through Tim's body. They were ready for the second half . . .

Were Germany?

43
WORLD CUP FINAL: ENGLAND V GERMANY (SECOND HALF)

Geoff Coren looked on in disbelief as the entire England team retook the field. Not one of them had been substituted. He couldn't believe his lasagne trick hadn't worked. He had added so much poison, they should have been going to the toilet for weeks. He tried to disguise his obvious anger. It was his secret and his alone.

England were fired up by the half-time team talk. Cruncher had a shot from twenty-five yards that whistled past the post; Goal Machine had two point-blank headers saved by Torstooper; Chaz Steakhouse had a low shot cleared off the line; and T. J. Wilkinson hit the crossbar with a stinging volley. The England fans in the crowd were buzzing with delight. England were on top and putting loads of pressure on the German goal.

Then, in the sixty-eighth minute, England won a

corner. Both teams flooded into the box. There was definitely a sense around the ground that this was going to be a crucial moment. T. J. Wilkinson took the corner, arching the ball expertly into the area and right on to the nose of Goal Machine. All he had to do was nod towards the net and the deadlock would be broken.

Just as he was about to finish the job, and wheel away to celebrate (chew some grass), an almighty gloved fist came flying out of a ruck of bodies and clouted the ball as far away from the penalty area as possible. It was Torstooper with another vital save.

The ball bounced once, about ten yards outside the penalty area, and was collected by the German striker Apfel, who was incredibly fast. He took off into the England half of the pitch, hopped over a tackle from Sid Melonhead and powered his way towards the area. Ludo left his six-yard box to close down the angle, but it wasn't enough. Apfel wasn't only really quick, he was a deadly finisher. He looped the ball over Ludo's head and into the back of the net, where it smacked Motorway on her bottom, causing her to let out a loud bleat. Apfel took off to celebrate, doing a swan dive towards the corner flag, where he was mobbed by his teammates.

ENGLAND 0 – 1 GERMANY

Tim sank to his knees. All that effort, and they had been beaten by a classic counter-attack goal.

'Twenty minutes left, laddie,' said McCloud with a grim look on his face. 'We've been applying all the pressure, we can't let up. Especially as we've been so close to scoring.'

Something had to give, and in the seventy-eighth minute, it did. Lightning received the ball on the halfway line and began a speedy scampering run down the right-hand side of the pitch. She dodged two sliding tackles, nipped past the German right back and zipped into their box. As usual, Torstooper was quickest to react and he left his goal line to pounce on the ball. The German defenders began clearing their lines, safe in the knowledge that their keeper had gobbled up the ball. But this time he hadn't! Lightning had put so much spin on the ball that Torstooper uncharacteristically dropped it, straight into the path of Goal Machine, who casually steered the ball into the back of the net from eight yards out.

ENGLAND 1 – 1 GERMANY

The fans and players on the pitch went bonkers. Tim, Cairo and McCloud ran on to the pitch and did knee slides down the touchline. Even Captain

Kneeslide did a knee slide, watching TV in his office at the prison.

Goal Machine just stood there. He could have had a tiny smile on his face, I'm not quite sure. T. J. Wilkinson went up to him and patted him carefully on the back. As everyone celebrated around him, Torstooper stood in his six-yard box, with his hands on his hips. He couldn't remember the last time he had dropped the ball. He never made goalkeeping mistakes like that.

High in the stand among all the dignitaries, celebrities and watermelon munchers sat Heinrich Prussia, with his head in his hands. He knew this time would come – it happens to everyone. All the greats eventually start to lose their touch, the older they get. Why did it have to happen in the World Cup final?

Torstooper managed to compose himself for the final twelve minutes, bravely stopping Goal Machine from giving England the lead with several more excellent saves.

Tim, McCloud, Cairo, Geoff Coren, the fans and everyone at home checked their watches. Not long left now. Surely this game was going to go to extra time. Coren continued to shake his head. Why hadn't any of the England players gone to the toilet yet? Someone must have stopped them from eating the lasagne. He looked over at the England bench and scowled. Who had ruined his brilliant plan?

44
WORLD CUP FINAL: ENGLAND V GERMANY (EXTRA TIME)

Nobody really enjoys extra time. The teams hate it because they are exhausted from the previous ninety minutes, the fans hate it because it's another thirty minutes of frantic worry, and people who don't support either team hate it because they want to watch something else.

Tim had to make substitutions in extra time. It was getting very hot in the stadium and some of the team were really huffing and puffing.

'Pick ones who are good at penalties,' said McCloud, covering his mouth so only Tim could hear. 'I've got a feeling this one could go all the way. Both sets of players are running on empty.'

Tim didn't think his nerves could handle it.

As the whistle blew for the start of extra time, the two sides slogged it out in the afternoon heat, but their legs felt like jelly strapped into concrete boots. It wasn't a pretty sight.

Passes went astray, players fell over the ball, long-range shots crashed high into the stands, and by the end of the thirty minutes, they were all totally puffed out, even the llamas.

The ref blew his whistle. The final had ended in a draw: 1 – 1. Penalties loomed.

Tim's stomach lurched about like a monster on a bouncy castle. His hands, feet and back were so sweaty it was unbearable.

In the opposing dugout, Geoff Coren finally peeled himself off his leather seat. His lasagne plan clearly hadn't worked and he was fuming. His career now relied on penalties and his players being able to get the ball past a llama, easily his most hated animal – apart from the giraffe that ate his ice cream when he went to a zoo last year. Plus, they are really tall, and he didn't like tall things.

'Right then,' said McCloud, clapping his hands together. He also looked a little green in the face. 'Time to pick our penalty takers. The ref wants the list. Who is up for it?'

A handful of brave players raised their hands.

Goal Machine, Lightning and Cruncher would also take one each.

The ref blew his whistle, sending Torstooper to wait by the side of the pitch, and Ludo and Motorway into the goal. He called forward the first penalty taker. It was the German striker Franz Apfel. Luckily for us, most of the German team were named after fruit. If you are too nervous to watch the penalties, try and work out which fruits they are.

Apfel, Melonhead, Kirsche, Steakhouse and Erdbeere stepped up to take the first five penalties. All of them cooly slotted home. Ludo and Torstooper didn't stand a chance.

3 – 2 to Germany. Cruncher was up next to take England's third.

Back in the dugout, Tim had covered his face with his hands, leaving a tiny gap between his fingers to peak out. Cairo had put a bucket over his head and was humming loudly. Only McCloud was standing to face the full force of the penalty stress, muttering under his breath, 'Smack it, smack it, smack it . . .'

Cruncher was super-powerful, but had very little control on his penalties. It was going one of two ways: thrashed into the top of the net, or high into the stands. The crowd held its collective breath . . .

Yes! Torstooper would have had his head torn off if he'd tried to stop that.

3 – 3

No problem for Germany's fourth, by Birne (that's a tough one, fruit-game fans), casually rolled into the right corner of the net.

4 – 3

Lightning was up next for England . . .

Tim had joined Cairo under the bucket. He couldn't take it any more.

And Lightning . . . SCORED! She made it look easy, straight down the middle.

4 – 4

Germany's left back, Traube, was their last to face the penalty lottery. He was easily the most anxious of all the takers. He repositioned the ball three times, fiddled with his socks and the top of his shorts, then nervously stared at the ref before the whistle was blown.

'Miss, miss, miss . . .' chanted McCloud under his breath.

Traube's run-up looked all wrong as he approached the ball. His shot was far too powerful, and it soared high above the goal and out over the top of the stadium. A spectacular miss, and the crowd went wild. If you look up in the sky now, you might be able to see it still flying through the air.

If England scored the next penalty, they would win the World Cup!

Goal Machine was going to take the fifth penalty. He strolled up to the penalty area as though he was on a casual walk in the countryside. He didn't know the whole world had stopped what they were doing to watch this momentous match. A silence fell over the stadium and the England team. Everyone held their breath.

Tim covered his eyes with his hands, then uncovered his eyes. He couldn't decide what to do.

His tummy was doing every single dance you can think of.

Goal Machine wandered up to the penalty spot, occasionally taking a nibble of the grass around him. He didn't look bothered in the slightest. Torstooper was primed and ready. He knew this was the biggest moment of his long and distinguished career. He had to save it.

The ref blew his whistle and Goal Machine cantered towards the ball. *He's going right*, thought Torstooper, and it certainly looked that way. Goal Machine reached the ball and Torstooper took off. Goal Machine stopped dead and lazily chipped the ball straight down the middle. It rose briefly in the air and then floated gently towards the net. Torstooper had already committed himself to diving right and had no chance of getting back and stopping it. The ball floated across the line: the bravest penalty ever, and Goal Machine had pulled it off!

5 – 4

England had done it.

ENGLAND HAD WON THE WORLD CUP.

45
THE AFTERMATH

For Tim, everything went into slow motion. McCloud, Cairo, all the subs, the rest of the backroom staff and what seemed like most of the England fans sprinted on to the pitch and began dancing and celebrating with the players. Tim just stood there, hardly able to move. It was if a lightning bolt had hit him. Out of the corner of his eye he could see Geoff Coren going through a range of emotions, before, crying like a baby, he finally stalked down the tunnel back to the German dressing room. His hair was as flat as a pancake. Just watching the celebrations unfold in front of him was perfect for Tim. Then a huge bucket of ice water was dumped on his head by a laughing Cairo and McCloud, and that woke him up. It was time to party.

When everything settled down and the fans had returned to their seats, it was time for the presentation of the trophy. The German team were first up to receive their runners-up medals, the medal that nobody wants. They shook hands with all the important people handing out the medals and then gloomily stood and clapped their opponents. Geoff Coren was nowhere to be seen.

Cairo found himself standing next to Torstooper, who looked incredibly glum.

'Bad luck, Dad,' said Cairo, holding out his hand for a handshake.

'The best team won,' replied Torstooper graciously. 'Torstooper doesn't want a handshake.'

'Oh, sorry,' said Cairo. His heart crushed itself into a little ball.

'Your *dad* wants a hug!' said the big German, and he grabbed Cairo, lifted him off his feet and gave him the best hug a dad could ever give. Cairo felt like he had just walked on the moon.

It was England's turn to go up and collect the trophy, and the players all agreed that Tim should be first to lift it.

Tim climbed the stairs with his team behind him. There it sat, glinting in the warm afternoon sun, and the lovely Princess Candice was there to hand it over. Behind her was Tim's family, cheering and clapping. He'd never seen them so happy. Even Fiona was smiling. Princess Candice passed the trophy over to Tim and gave him a huge smile.

'Congratulations, Tim,' she said. 'This is the best day ever.'

Tim could hear the crowd noise swelling behind him. He turned and lifted the golden trophy high over his head and the place erupted, camera lights flashed, fireworks exploded above the stadium and glittering confetti belched out of huge confetti cannons.

The England team started bouncing and singing alongside him. Out on the pitch stood four llamas and a sheep munching on the centre circle, away from all the fuss. Only one of them was looking up at him. It was Ludo. It looked like he was nodding his approval.

46
BACK HOME

The next two days were a total blur for the entire England team. They landed at the airport in London and were immediately taken on a tour of the whole country on an open-topped bus. All eleven llamas were driven behind in a huge trailer. They didn't really know what was going on, but it seemed like a lot of fun. Everyone came out of their houses to clap and cheer, even people who still didn't like football.

Then they were taken to the huge palace where the Royal Family lived, and the entire team were all given knighthoods, even the llamas. It would now be Sir Tim, Sir Cairo, Sir Cruncher, Sir Goal Machine, Sir Ludo, Dame Lightning and Princess Motorway, although of course she already thought she was one. Even McCloud was made a Sir, but he only agreed as long as he could still live in his caravan.

Karl-Heinz Torstooper came to watch the

ceremony and told his son how proud of him he was, which to Cairo was better than any knighthood. Torstooper had sacked Prussia after the final and decided he didn't want his son to go through what he had as a teenager. Prussia wasn't very happy, but that hasn't stopped him; he's now searching the world for the next greatest footballer. Be careful he doesn't find you.

After the ceremony Molly nervously approached Karl-Heinz Torstooper and they had their first chat in over twelve years. I'm not telling you what was said – it's private.

As for Geoff Coren, he was sacked by Germany. After the game he went into the German changing room and in a huge rage started smashing up the place. He also drank all the champagne he could find and got very drunk. Then he found some food hidden under some foil and began devouring it. He was very hungry. It was only after he peeled back a bit more of the foil that he realized what it was: a giant lasagne. A giant poisonous lasagne! As far as I'm aware, he's still in the Big Sparkly Diamond Stadium toilets.

Back at the farm, once everything had calmed down, Sir Tim and Sir Cairo sat toasting marshmallows on the fire. Tim wasn't the biggest fan of toasted marshmallows, but this seemed to be a thing they both did after a big Cup final.

'That's it then, is it?' said Cairo.

'That's what then?' replied Tim.

'You know, the end. We've won the World Cup. Doesn't that mean we've won football?'

'The end?' replied Tim in disbelief. 'Football never ends. It goes on forever, it never stops. There will be another World Cup in four years.'

'Oh,' said Cairo, disappointed. 'This never happens with hedgehog racing. I don't think I'll ever understand football.'

'I don't think I'll ever understand it either,' said Tim. 'It's the best sport ever and I'll still always love it. There's ups and downs, so having your friends and family around you to experience it is really the best thing ever.'

Cairo nodded. 'I don't think I can go through penalties again. Do you think being a vet or a zoo keeper would be less stressful?'

'What kind of vet?'

'I dunno . . . Maybe a like a big cat one. Things with claws and sharp teeth.'

'Think I'd rather do the penalties again,' said Tim.

So that's the story of the llamas at the World Cup, and once again it wouldn't have happened without me. England are the World Champions, which hasn't happened in a staggeringly long time. It just goes to show you should never give up, whatever obstacles are thrown in your way.

Now, where's my chocolate mousse?

ACKNOWLEDGEMENTS

Big thanks:

To my brilliant editor, Lucy Pearse. Her advice, support and suggestions have been crucial to making *Llamas Go Large* the story it is today. I'm a very headphones-on–shut-the-world-out kind of writer, so only a tiny handful of people are privy to my witterings. Thankfully Lucy understood what I was rattling on about and was on hand to steer me in the right direction. And thank you to everyone at Macmillan Children's Books for their continued support.

To my superstar agent, Gemma Cooper, who once again has been a brilliant sounding board and savvy judge and to Sarah Horne, the illustrator of the Llama United books, who has brought the characters to life in a fantastic way.

To the unfortunate people who have to live with me – Gwen, Spike and Zach. I know working in the room where the Playstation lives is incredibly unpopular but thanks for allowing me the time to shut myself away in there for hours on end. Pablo the cat – your indifference to all the ideas that I've talked to you about has been incredibly helpful. The rest of my family, who fortunately don't have to live with me, especially Mum, Zoe, Sally, Ashley, Rosie, Morgan and Haydn.

To various groups of friends who are always keen to know how I'm getting on and have supported Llama United from day one. Thanks, in no particular order, to the Sowood Street boys, the Diagonal Tigers, the ex-Orange chumps, the Wigton Mums and Dads, the Luton massive, the Golden Triangle adventurers, everyone at STRI and finally all the book-type people I've met over the last year. You are all brilliant.

Finally a big thanks to my Germanic inspiration, the Russ family. Guy, Tim, Peter and not forgetting the much missed Doris. Without you we'd be a few characters short in *Llamas Go Large*, and I'd have never gone to Nork if you didn't live there.

I'm not thanking football this time round, because it's been an awful season . . . again.

C'mon you Irons.

ABOUT THE AUTHOR

Scott Allen was brought up in the horse-racing town of Epsom. After discovering he was too tall and heavy to be a jockey, he turned his attention to football. He is a professional sports writer, editor and digital-content specialist. Scott now lives in Yorkshire with his wife, two children and cat. His first novel, *Llama United* was selected for the Reading Agency's 2017 Summer Reading Challenge. He is a West Ham supporter, but we don't hold that against him.

ABOUT THE ILLUSTRATOR

Sarah Horne grew up in snowy Derbyshire, UK, with some goats and a brother.

Alongside working on some very funny children's titles, Sarah has also worked on commissions for the *Guardian*, the *Sunday Times*, Kew Gardens, *Sesame Street* and for IKEA as their Children's Illustrator In Residence.

She now draws, paints, writes and giggles from underneath a pile of paper at her studio in London.

What happens when eleven llamas unknowingly eat the ashes of one of the greatest footballers of all time . . . ?

Llama United, of course!